# THE CALL OF THE WILD

## JACK LONDON

CAMPFIRE®

KALYANI NAVYUG MEDIA PVT LTD

# THE CALL OF THE WILD

Wordsmith: Lloyd S. Wagner
Illustrator: Sachin Nagar
Colorist: Pradeep Sherawat

Cover Artist: Sachin Nagar

CAMPFIRE®

www.campfire.co.in

**Mission Statement**

To entertain and educate young minds by creating unique illustrated books that recount stories of human values, arouse curiosity in the world around us, and inspire with tales of great deeds of unforgettable people.

Published by Kalyani Navyug Media Pvt Ltd
101 C, Shiv House, Hari Nagar Ashram, New Delhi 110014, India

ISBN: 978-93-80028-33-0



First Published 2010
Eighth Impression 2020

## About the Author

Jack London, whose real name was John Griffith Chaney, was born on January 12, 1876 in San Francisco, USA. A resounding theme in his literary work was one of a struggle to survive. London's upbringing and his experiences in later life would serve as the grounding for his unique naturalistic style of writing. Deserted by his father, London was raised by his spiritualist mother who was known for her eccentricity. By the age of 14, London was developing a taste for adventure, and he left school to work for a government fish patrol. He would later join the navy, and would explore most of America by travelling as a hobo on freight trains. In 1897, Jack London traveled to the Klondike hoping to strike it rich in America's last gold rush. While he did not find gold in the harsh arctic wilderness, London did discover a wealth of material he would later fashion into two of his best known novels, *The Call of the Wild* and *White Fang*. Published in 1903, *The Call of the Wild* benefited from the rise of the modern press and publishing industry, becoming immensely popular and launching London's career. Over the following years, London wrote prolifically, drawing again on his Klondike adventure for *White Fang* and his experiences at sea as a young man for *The Sea Wolf*.

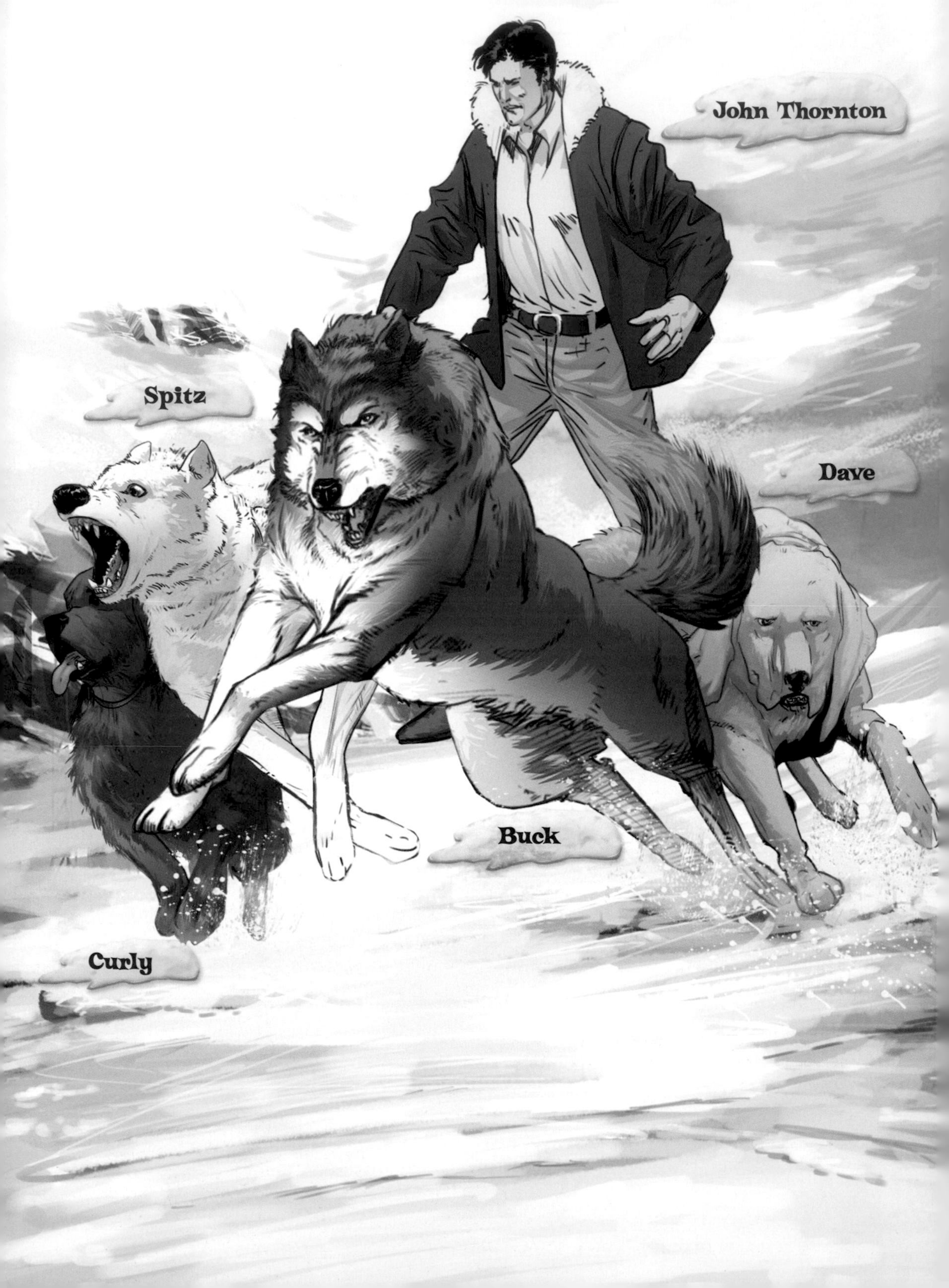
John Thornton
Spitz
Dave
Buck
Curly

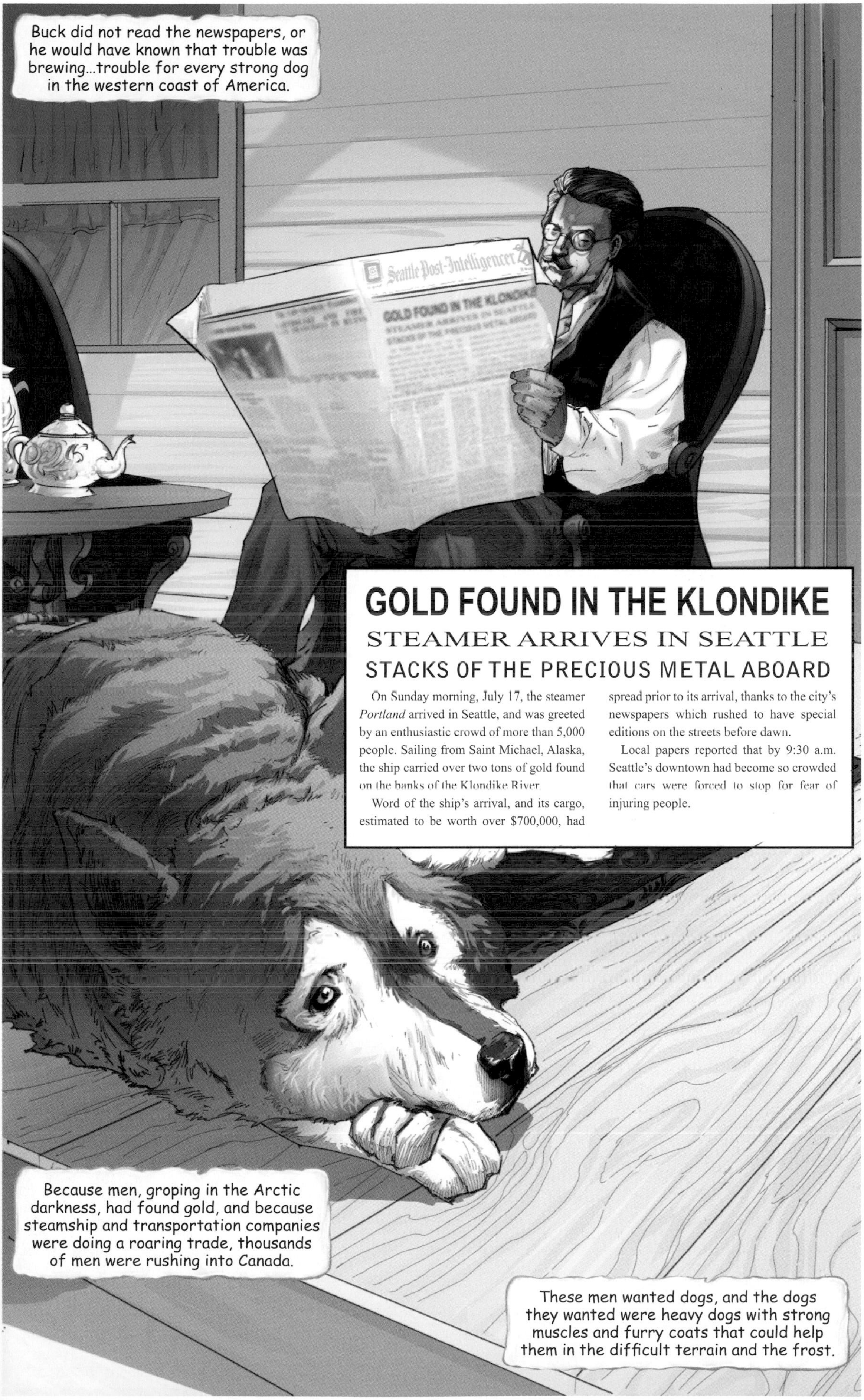
Buck did not read the newspapers, or he would have known that trouble was brewing...trouble for every strong dog in the western coast of America.
GOLD FOUND IN THE KLONDIKE
STEAMER ARRIVES IN SEATTLE
STACKS OF THE PRECIOUS METAL ABOARD
On Sunday morning, July 17, the steamer *Portland* arrived in Seattle, and was greeted by an enthusiastic crowd of more than 5,000 people. Sailing from Saint Michael, Alaska, the ship carried over two tons of gold found on the banks of the Klondike River.
Word of the ship's arrival, and its cargo, estimated to be worth over $700,000, had spread prior to its arrival, thanks to the city's newspapers which rushed to have special editions on the streets before dawn.
Local papers reported that by 9:30 a.m. Seattle's downtown had become so crowded that cars were forced to stop for fear of injuring people.
Because men, groping in the Arctic darkness, had found gold, and because steamship and transportation companies were doing a roaring trade, thousands of men were rushing into Canada.
These men wanted dogs, and the dogs they wanted were heavy dogs with strong muscles and furry coats that could help them in the difficult terrain and the frost.

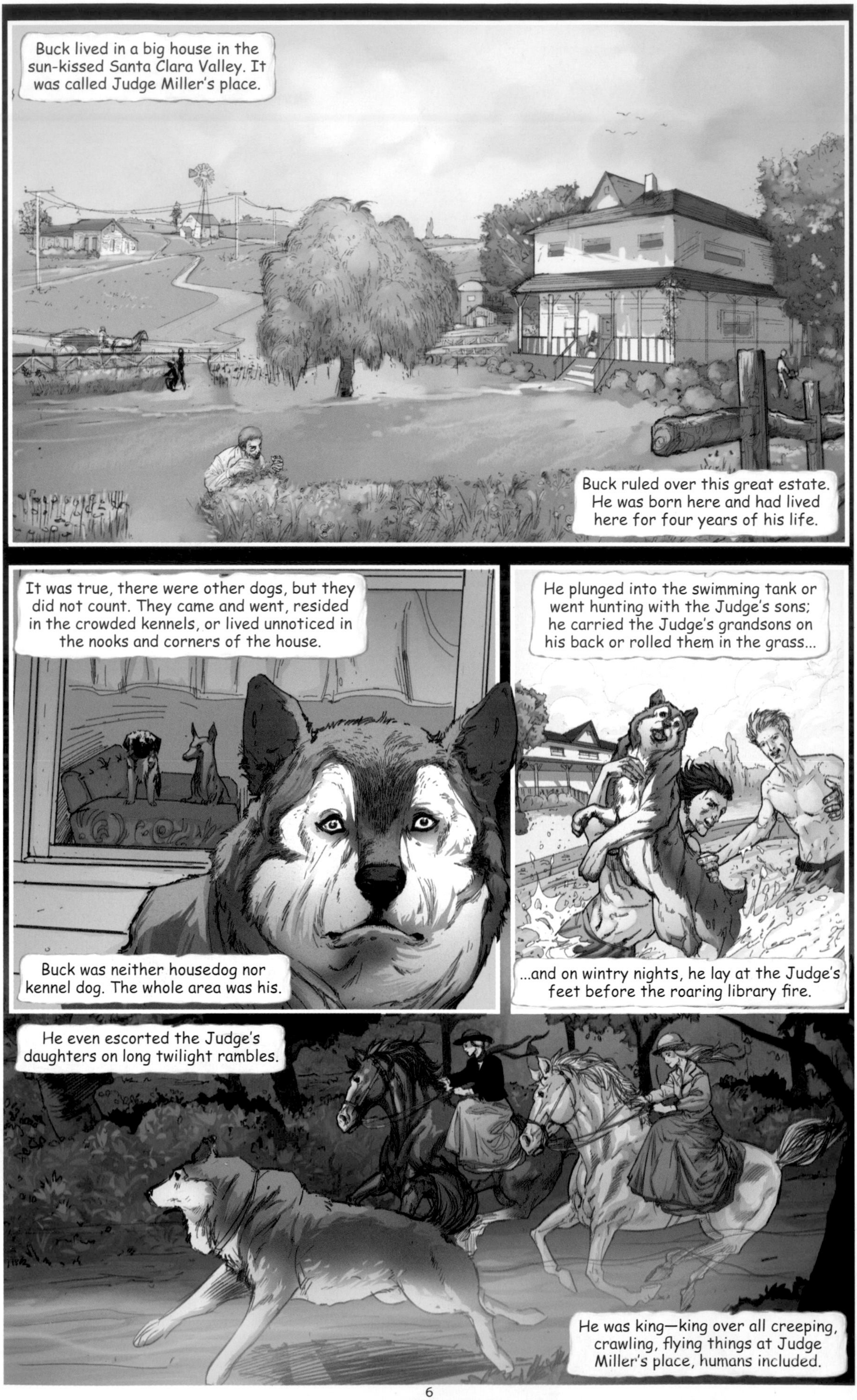
Buck lived in a big house in the sun-kissed Santa Clara Valley. It was called Judge Miller's place.
Buck ruled over this great estate. He was born here and had lived here for four years of his life.
It was true, there were other dogs, but they did not count. They came and went, resided in the crowded kennels, or lived unnoticed in the nooks and corners of the house.
Buck was neither housedog nor kennel dog. The whole area was his.
He plunged into the swimming tank or went hunting with the Judge's sons; he carried the Judge's grandsons on his back or rolled them in the grass...
...and on wintry nights, he lay at the Judge's feet before the roaring library fire.
He even escorted the Judge's daughters on long twilight rambles.
He was king—king over all creeping, crawling, flying things at Judge Miller's place, humans included.

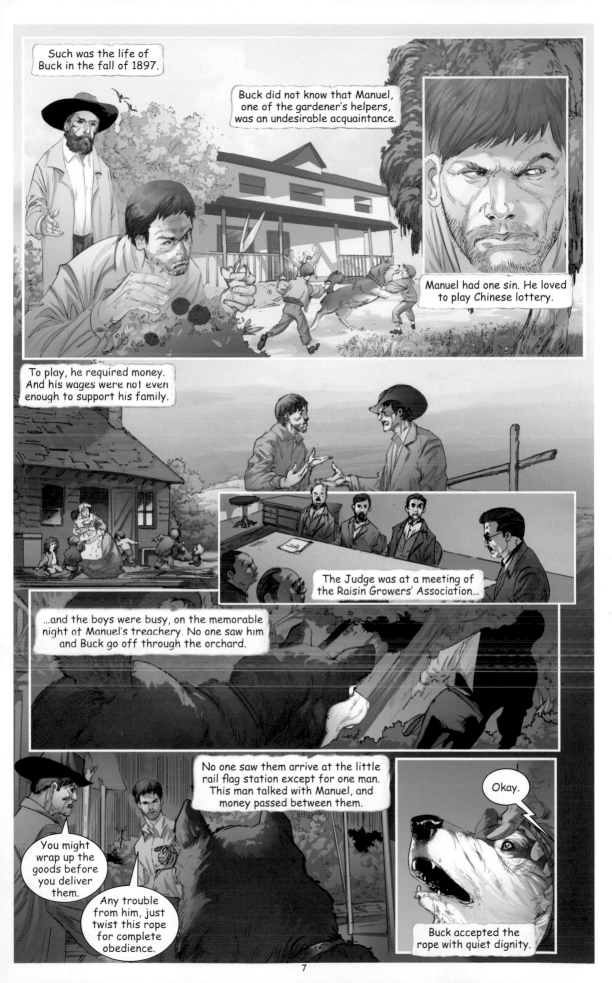

Such was the life of Buck in the fall of 1897.

Buck did not know that Manuel, one of the gardener's helpers, was an undesirable acquaintance.

Manuel had one sin. He loved to play Chinese lottery.

To play, he required money. And his wages were not even enough to support his family.

The Judge was at a meeting of the Raisin Growers' Association...

...and the boys were busy, on the memorable night of Manuel's treachery. No one saw him and Buck go off through the orchard.

No one saw them arrive at the little rail flag station except for one man. This man talked with Manuel, and money passed between them.

You might wrap up the goods before you deliver them.

Any trouble from him, just twist this rope for complete obedience.

Okay.

Buck accepted the rope with quiet dignity.

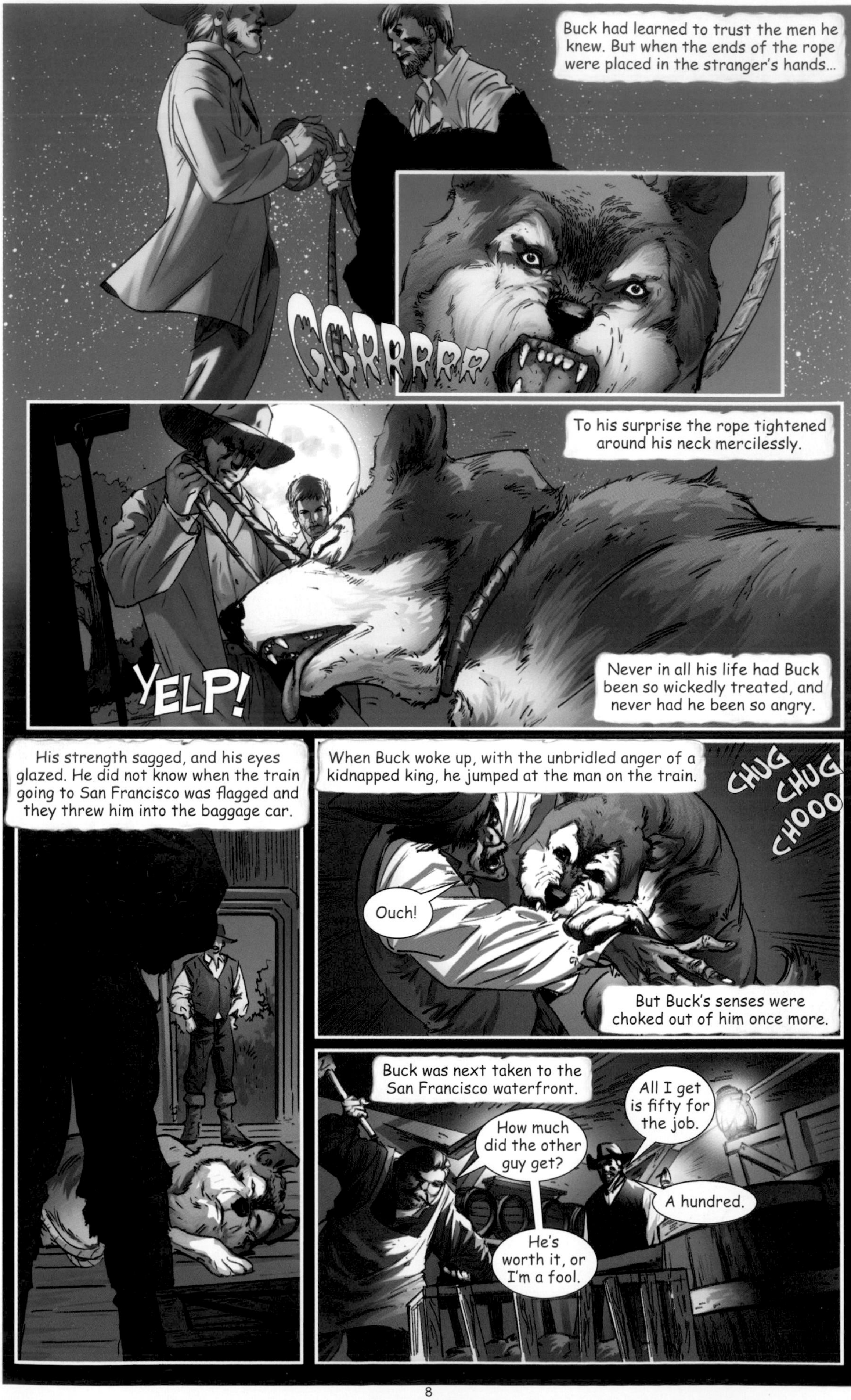

Buck had learned to trust the men he knew. But when the ends of the rope were placed in the stranger's hands...
GGRRRRRR
To his surprise the rope tightened around his neck mercilessly.
YELP!
Never in all his life had Buck been so wickedly treated, and never had he been so angry.
His strength sagged, and his eyes glazed. He did not know when the train going to San Francisco was flagged and they threw him into the baggage car.
When Buck woke up, with the unbridled anger of a kidnapped king, he jumped at the man on the train.
CHUG CHUG CHOOO
Ouch!
But Buck's senses were choked out of him once more.
Buck was next taken to the San Francisco waterfront.
All I get is fifty for the job.
How much did the other guy get?
A hundred.
He's worth it, or I'm a fool.

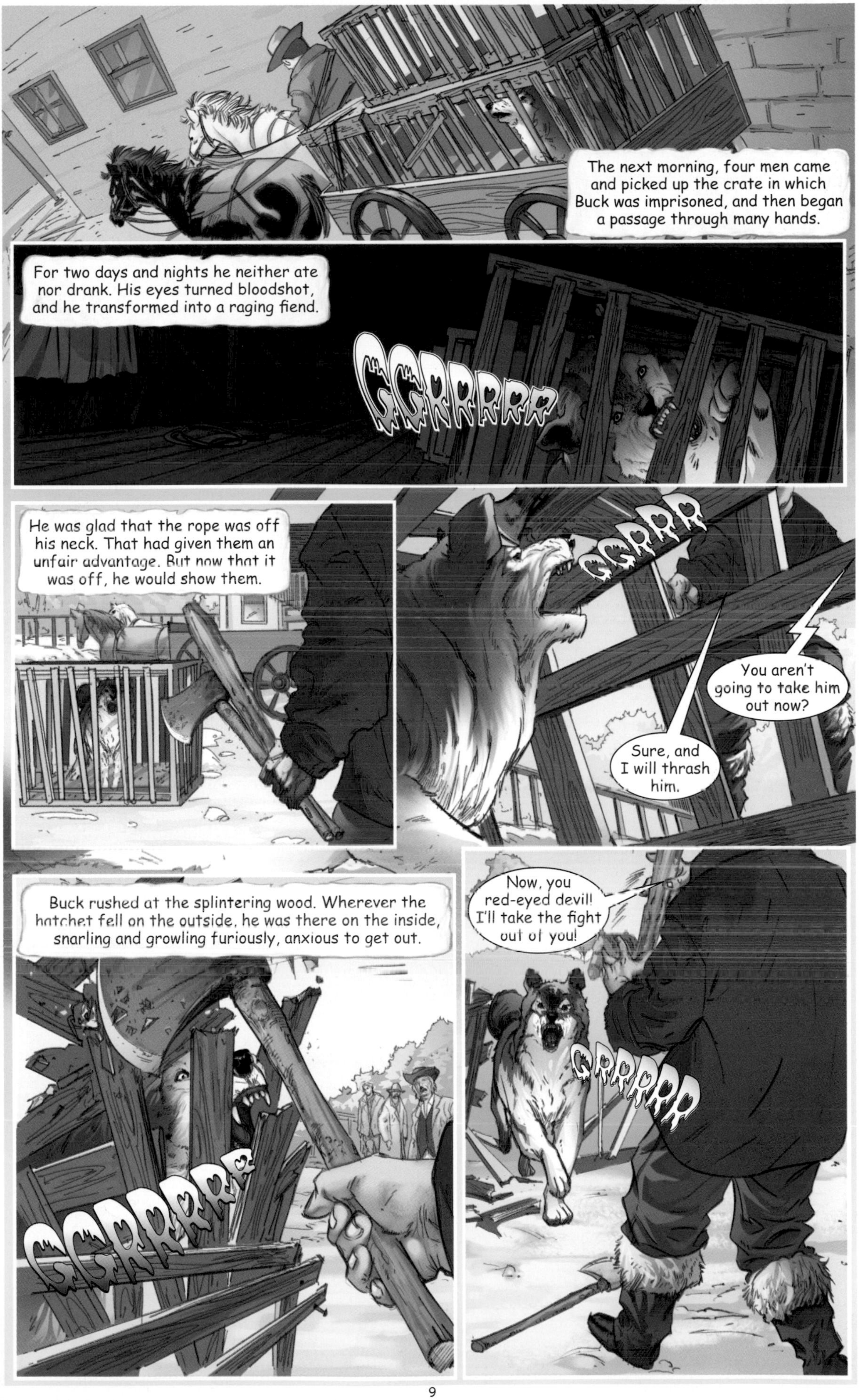
The next morning, four men came and picked up the crate in which Buck was imprisoned, and then began a passage through many hands.
For two days and nights he neither ate nor drank. His eyes turned bloodshot, and he transformed into a raging fiend.
GGRRRRRR
He was glad that the rope was off his neck. That had given them an unfair advantage. But now that it was off, he would show them.
GGRRR
You aren't going to take him out now?
Sure, and I will thrash him.
Buck rushed at the splintering wood. Wherever the hatchet fell on the outside, he was there on the inside, snarling and growling furiously, anxious to get out.
GGRRRRR
Now, you red-eyed devil! I'll take the fight out of you!
GRRRRR

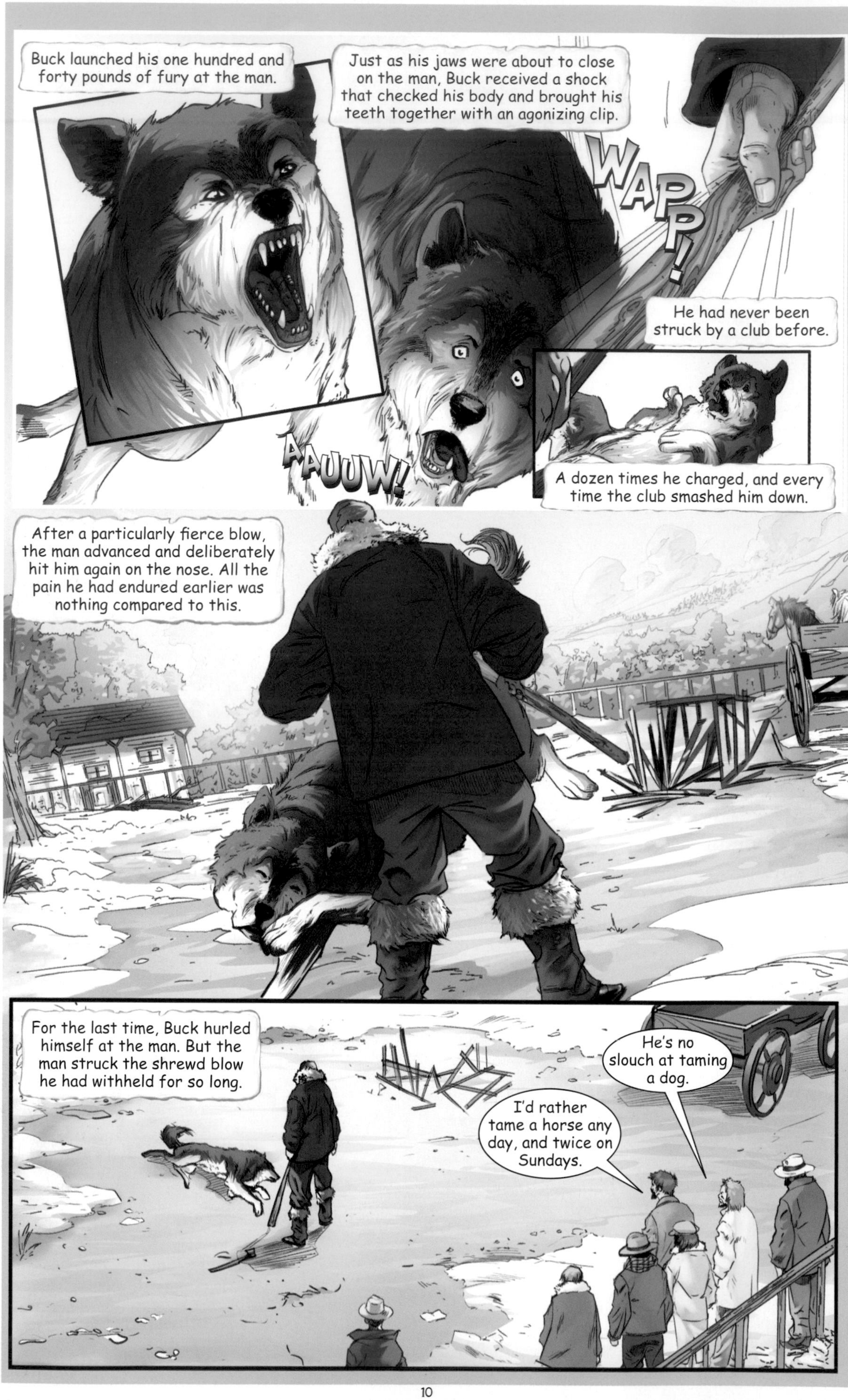

Buck launched his one hundred and forty pounds of fury at the man.
Just as his jaws were about to close on the man, Buck received a shock that checked his body and brought his teeth together with an agonizing clip.
WAPP!
AAUUW!
He had never been struck by a club before.
A dozen times he charged, and every time the club smashed him down.
After a particularly fierce blow, the man advanced and deliberately hit him again on the nose. All the pain he had endured earlier was nothing compared to this.
For the last time, Buck hurled himself at the man. But the man struck the shrewd blow he had withheld for so long.
He's no slouch at taming a dog.
I'd rather tame a horse any day, and twice on Sundays.

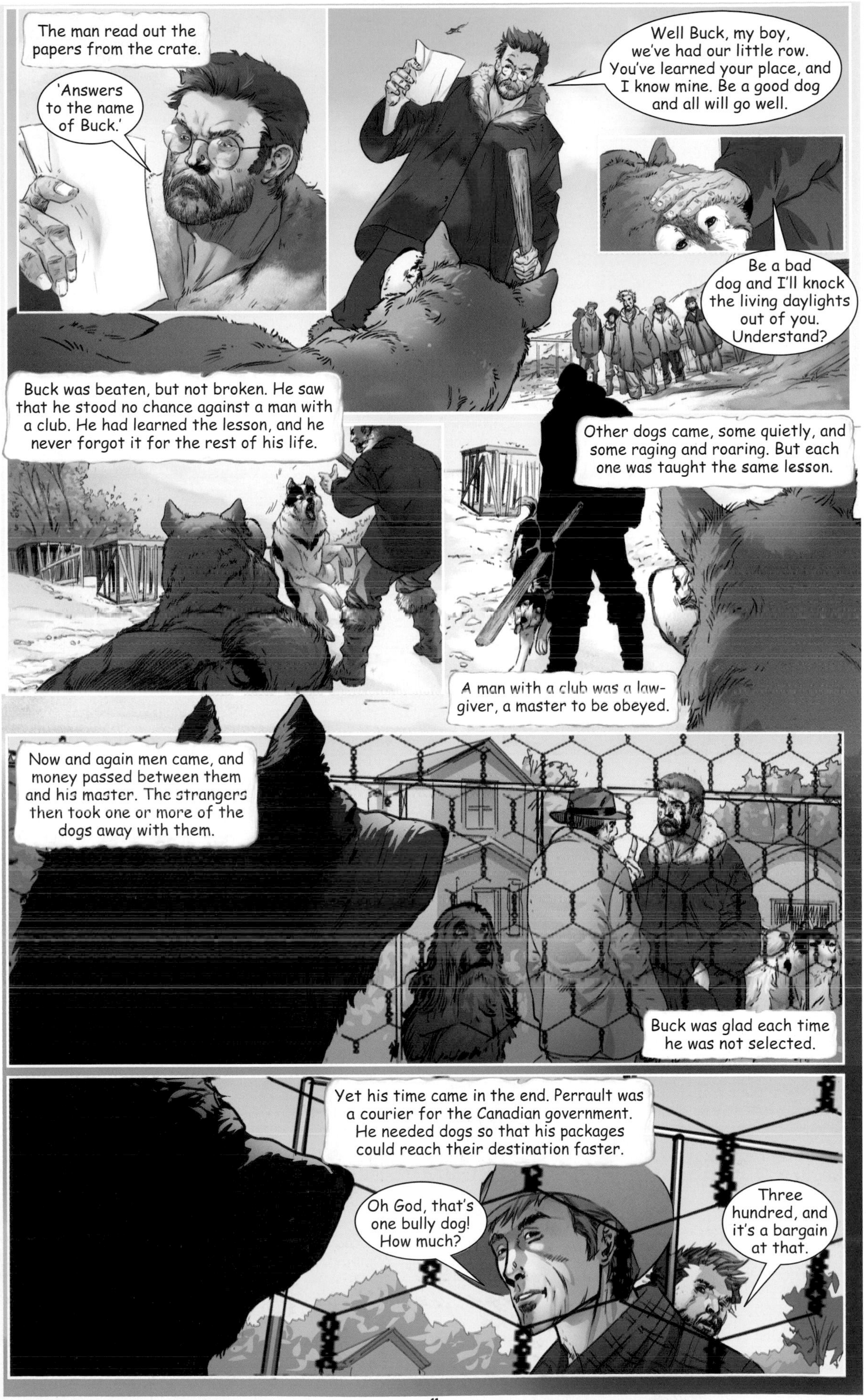
The man read out the papers from the crate.
'Answers to the name of Buck.'
Well Buck, my boy, we've had our little row. You've learned your place, and I know mine. Be a good dog and all will go well.
Be a bad dog and I'll knock the living daylights out of you. Understand?
Buck was beaten, but not broken. He saw that he stood no chance against a man with a club. He had learned the lesson, and he never forgot it for the rest of his life.
Other dogs came, some quietly, and some raging and roaring. But each one was taught the same lesson.
A man with a club was a law-giver, a master to be obeyed.
Now and again men came, and money passed between them and his master. The strangers then took one or more of the dogs away with them.
Buck was glad each time he was not selected.
Yet his time came in the end. Perrault was a courier for the Canadian government. He needed dogs so that his packages could reach their destination faster.
Oh God, that's one bully dog! How much?
Three hundred, and it's a bargain at that.

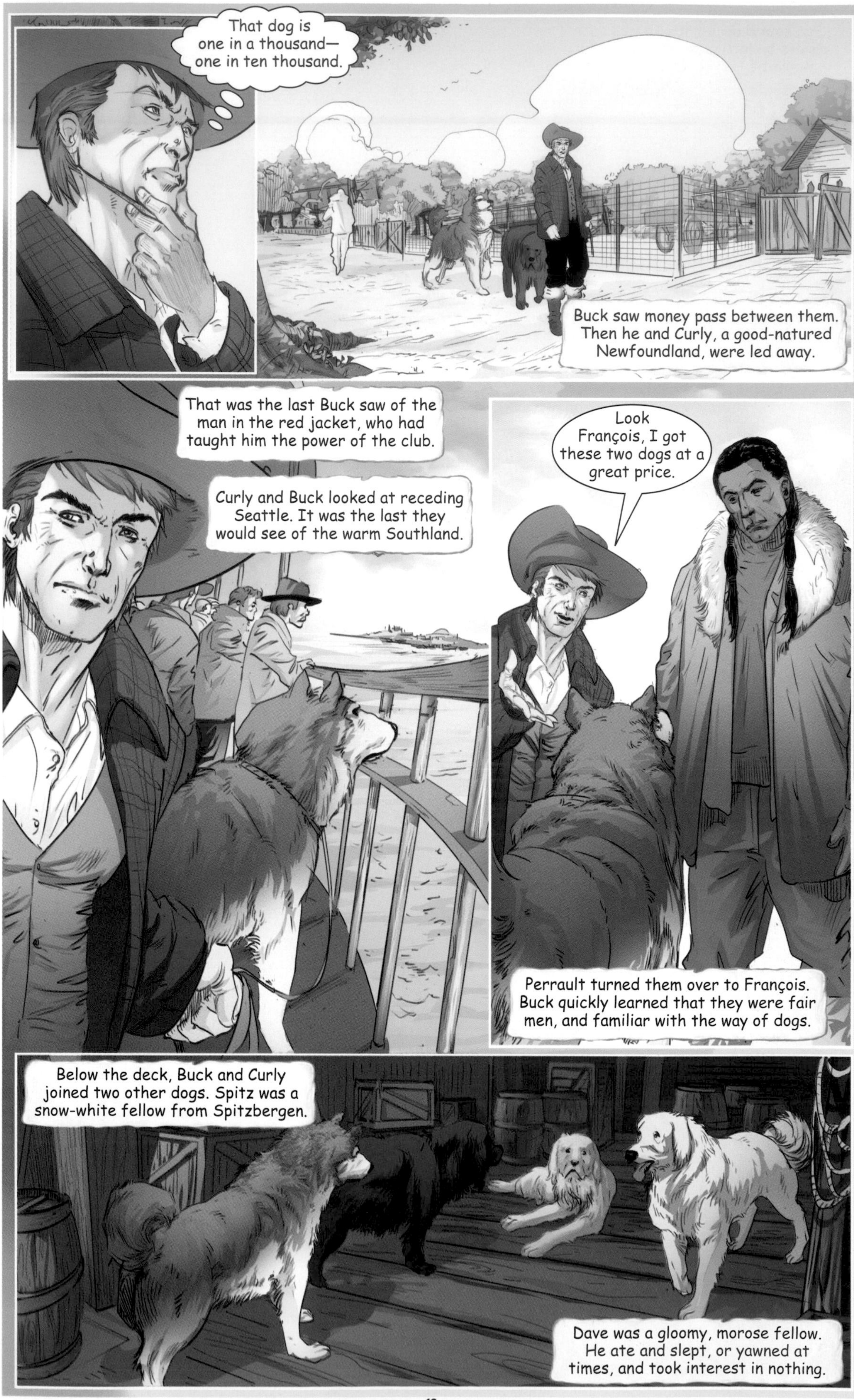
That dog is one in a thousand— one in ten thousand.
Buck saw money pass between them. Then he and Curly, a good-natured Newfoundland, were led away.
That was the last Buck saw of the man in the red jacket, who had taught him the power of the club.
Curly and Buck looked at receding Seattle. It was the last they would see of the warm Southland.
Look François, I got these two dogs at a great price.
Perrault turned them over to François. Buck quickly learned that they were fair men, and familiar with the way of dogs.
Below the deck, Buck and Curly joined two other dogs. Spitz was a snow-white fellow from Spitzbergen.
Dave was a gloomy, morose fellow. He ate and slept, or yawned at times, and took interest in nothing.

He showed Curly that all he wanted was to be left alone, and that there would be trouble if he were not.

GRRRR

Spitz, on the other hand, was friendly, but in a wicked way, smiling into one's face while he contemplated some underhand trick.

For instance, he stole Buck's food at the first meal.

CRACK!

As Buck sprang to punish him, François's whip sang through the air, reaching the culprit first.

All Buck had to do was take back his bone.

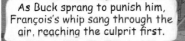

Buck decided that it was fair of François, and his opinion of him improved considerably.

Day and night, the ship's propeller throbbed away, and the weather steadily grew colder.

At last, one morning, the propeller was quiet, and change was at hand.

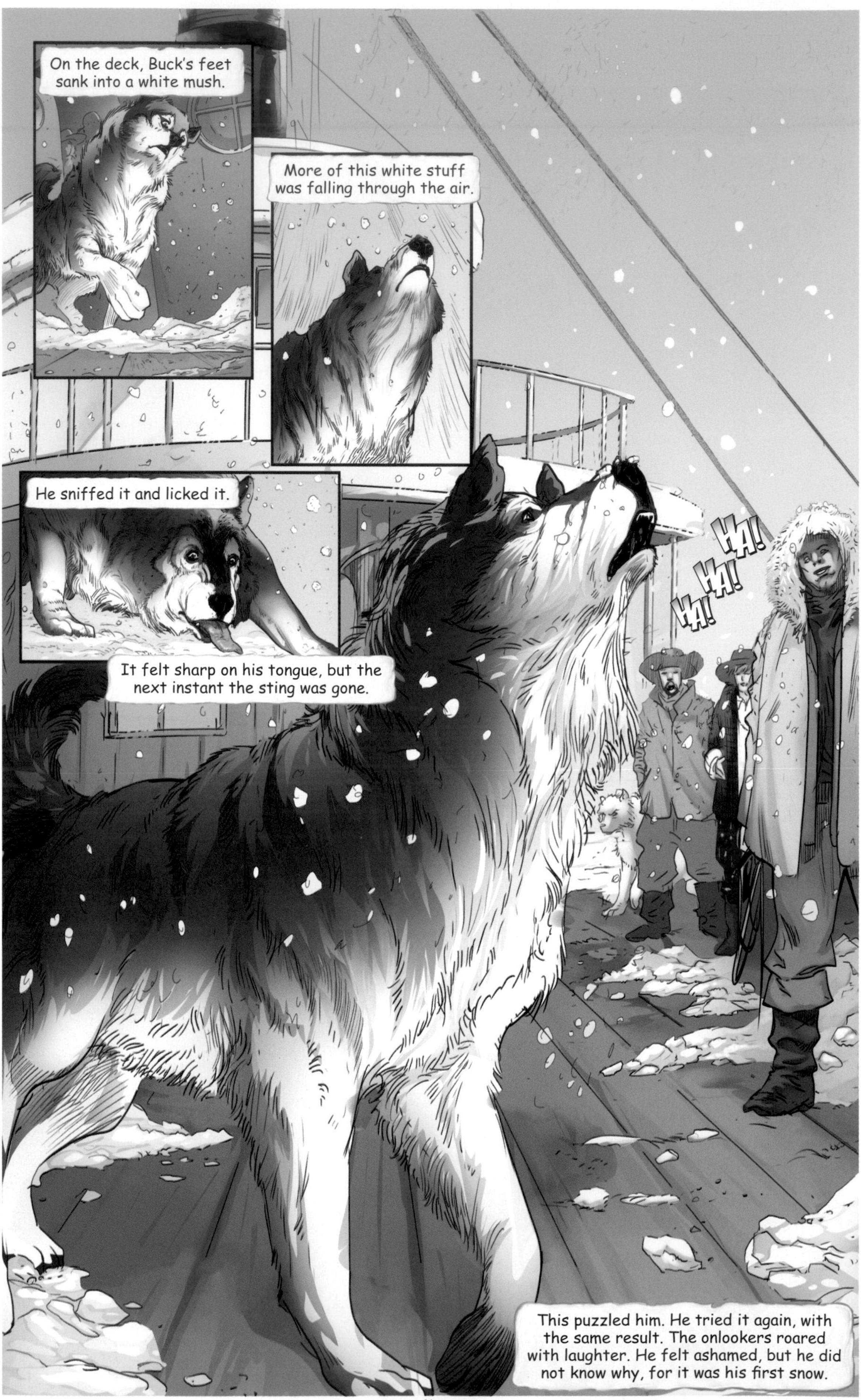
On the deck, Buck's feet sank into a white mush.
More of this white stuff was falling through the air.
He sniffed it and licked it.
It felt sharp on his tongue, but the next instant the sting was gone.
HA! HA! HA!
This puzzled him. He tried it again, with the same result. The onlookers roared with laughter. He felt ashamed, but he did not know why, for it was his first snow.

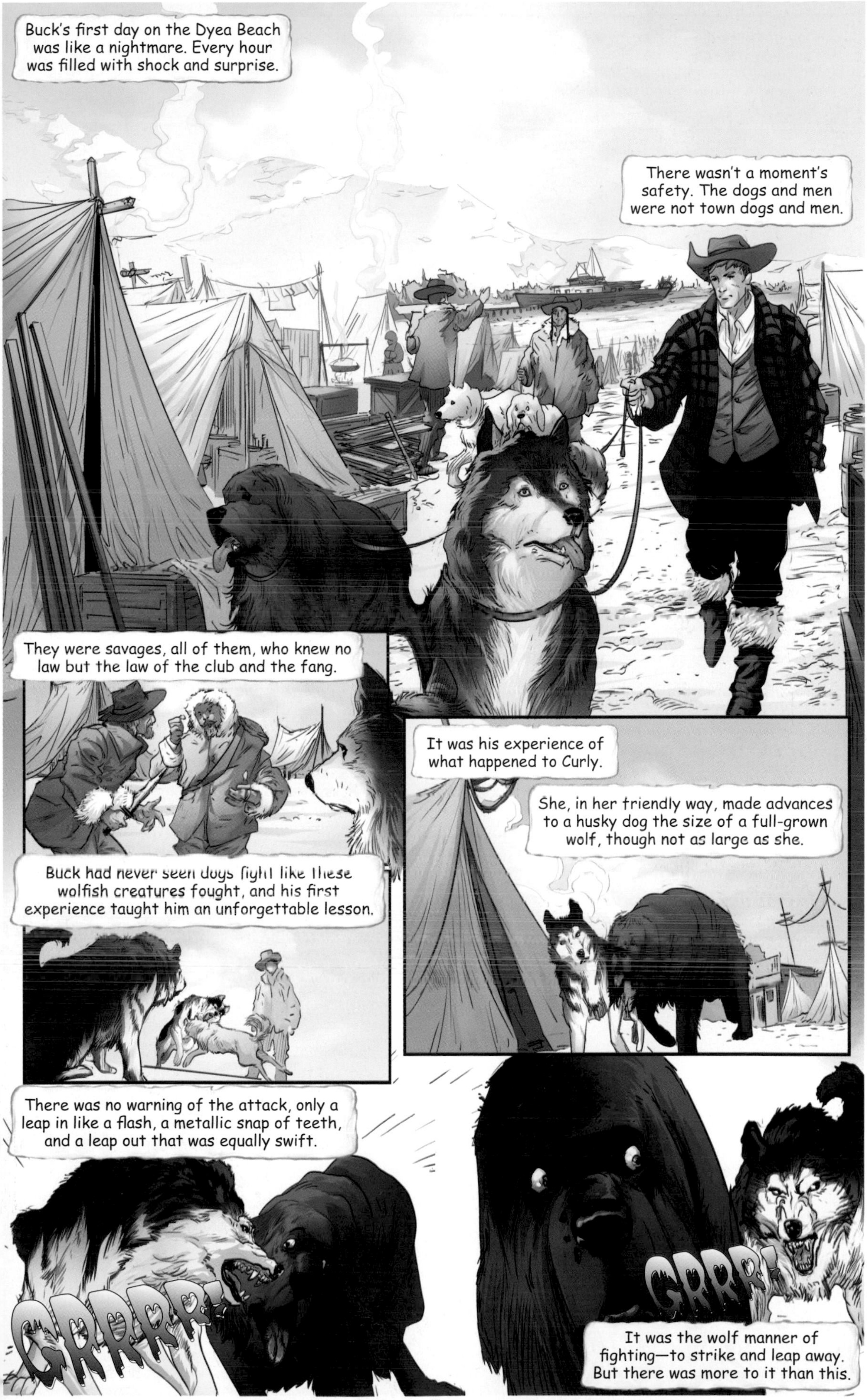
Buck's first day on the Dyea Beach was like a nightmare. Every hour was filled with shock and surprise.
There wasn't a moment's safety. The dogs and men were not town dogs and men.
They were savages, all of them, who knew no law but the law of the club and the fang.
Buck had never seen dogs fight like these wolfish creatures fought, and his first experience taught him an unforgettable lesson.
It was his experience of what happened to Curly.
She, in her friendly way, made advances to a husky dog the size of a full-grown wolf, though not as large as she.
There was no warning of the attack, only a leap in like a flash, a metallic snap of teeth, and a leap out that was equally swift.
GRRRR!
GRRR!
It was the wolf manner of fighting—to strike and leap away. But there was more to it than this.

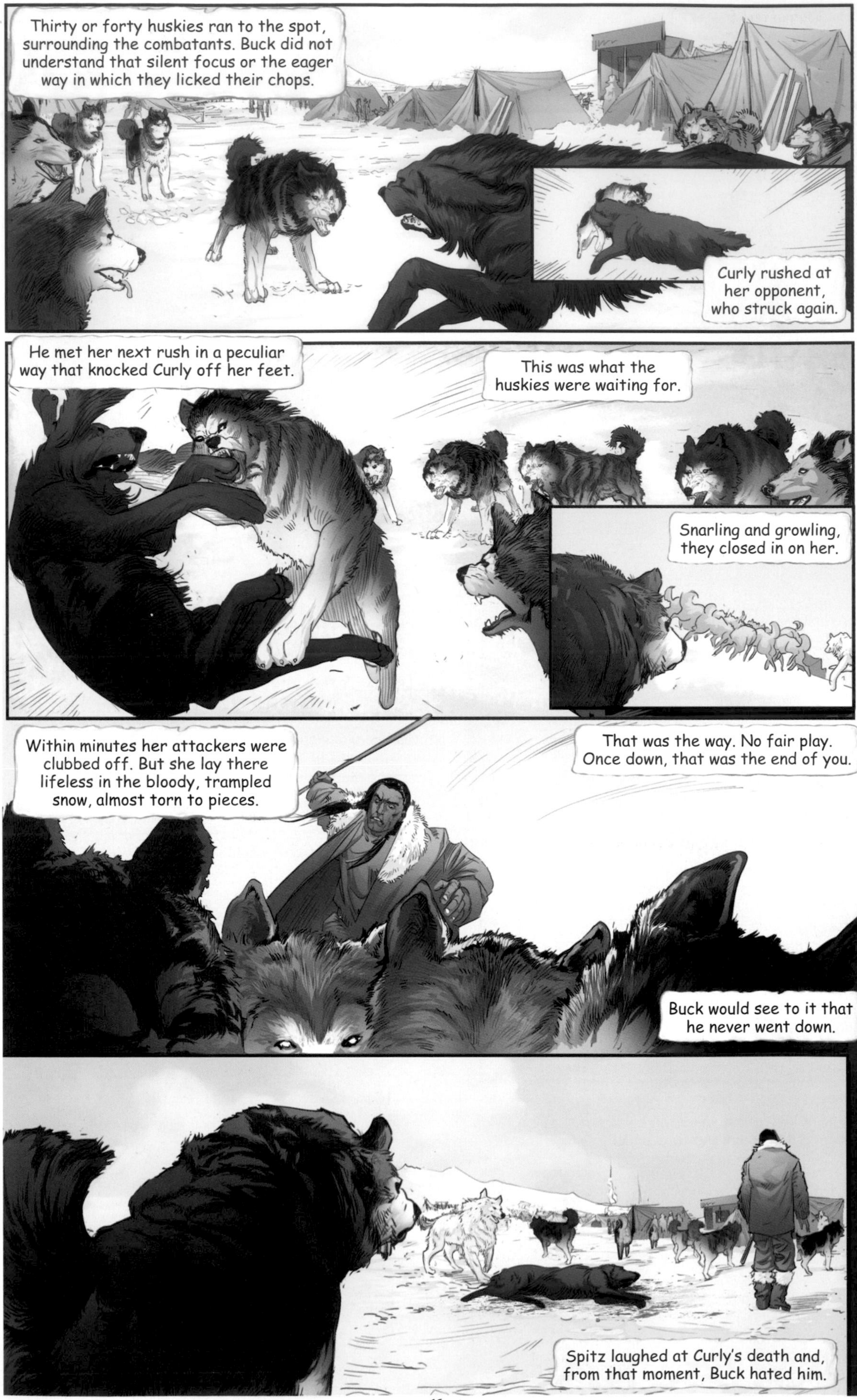
Thirty or forty huskies ran to the spot, surrounding the combatants. Buck did not understand that silent focus or the eager way in which they licked their chops.
Curly rushed at her opponent, who struck again.
He met her next rush in a peculiar way that knocked Curly off her feet.
This was what the huskies were waiting for.
Snarling and growling, they closed in on her.
Within minutes her attackers were clubbed off. But she lay there lifeless in the bloody, trampled snow, almost torn to pieces.
That was the way. No fair play. Once down, that was the end of you.
Buck would see to it that he never went down.
Spitz laughed at Curly's death and, from that moment, Buck hated him.

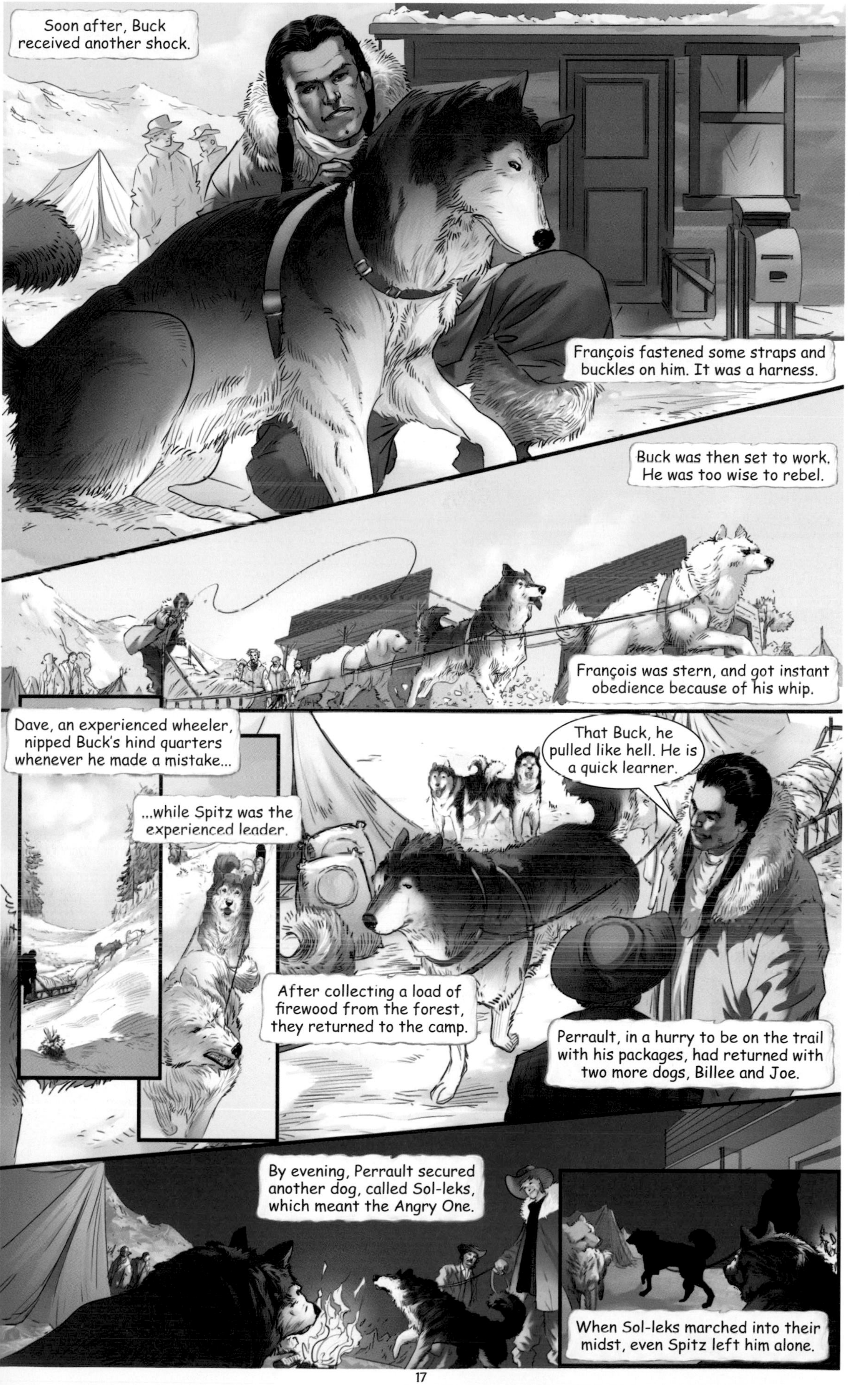
Soon after, Buck received another shock.
François fastened some straps and buckles on him. It was a harness.
Buck was then set to work. He was too wise to rebel.
François was stern, and got instant obedience because of his whip.
Dave, an experienced wheeler, nipped Buck's hind quarters whenever he made a mistake...
...while Spitz was the experienced leader.
After collecting a load of firewood from the forest, they returned to the camp.
That Buck, he pulled like hell. He is a quick learner.
Perrault, in a hurry to be on the trail with his packages, had returned with two more dogs, Billee and Joe.
By evening, Perrault secured another dog, called Sol-leks, which meant the Angry One.
When Sol-leks marched into their midst, even Spitz left him alone.

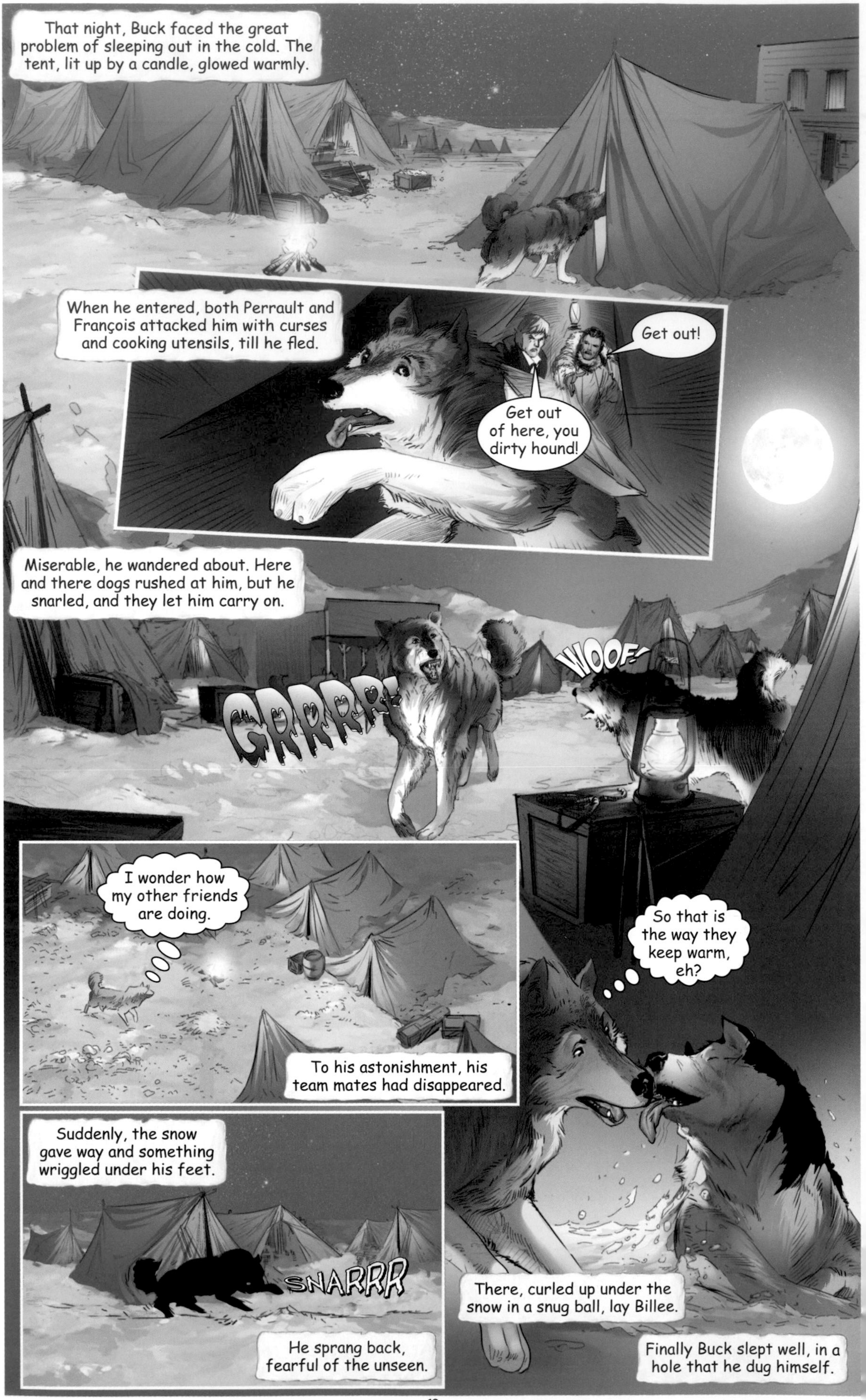
That night, Buck faced the great problem of sleeping out in the cold. The tent, lit up by a candle, glowed warmly.
When he entered, both Perrault and François attacked him with curses and cooking utensils, till he fled.
Get out!
Get out of here, you dirty hound!
Miserable, he wandered about. Here and there dogs rushed at him, but he snarled, and they let him carry on.
GRRRR!
WOOF!
I wonder how my other friends are doing.
To his astonishment, his team mates had disappeared.
Suddenly, the snow gave way and something wriggled under his feet.
SNARRR
He sprang back, fearful of the unseen.
So that is the way they keep warm, eh?
There, curled up under the snow in a snug ball, lay Billee.
Finally Buck slept well, in a hole that he dug himself.

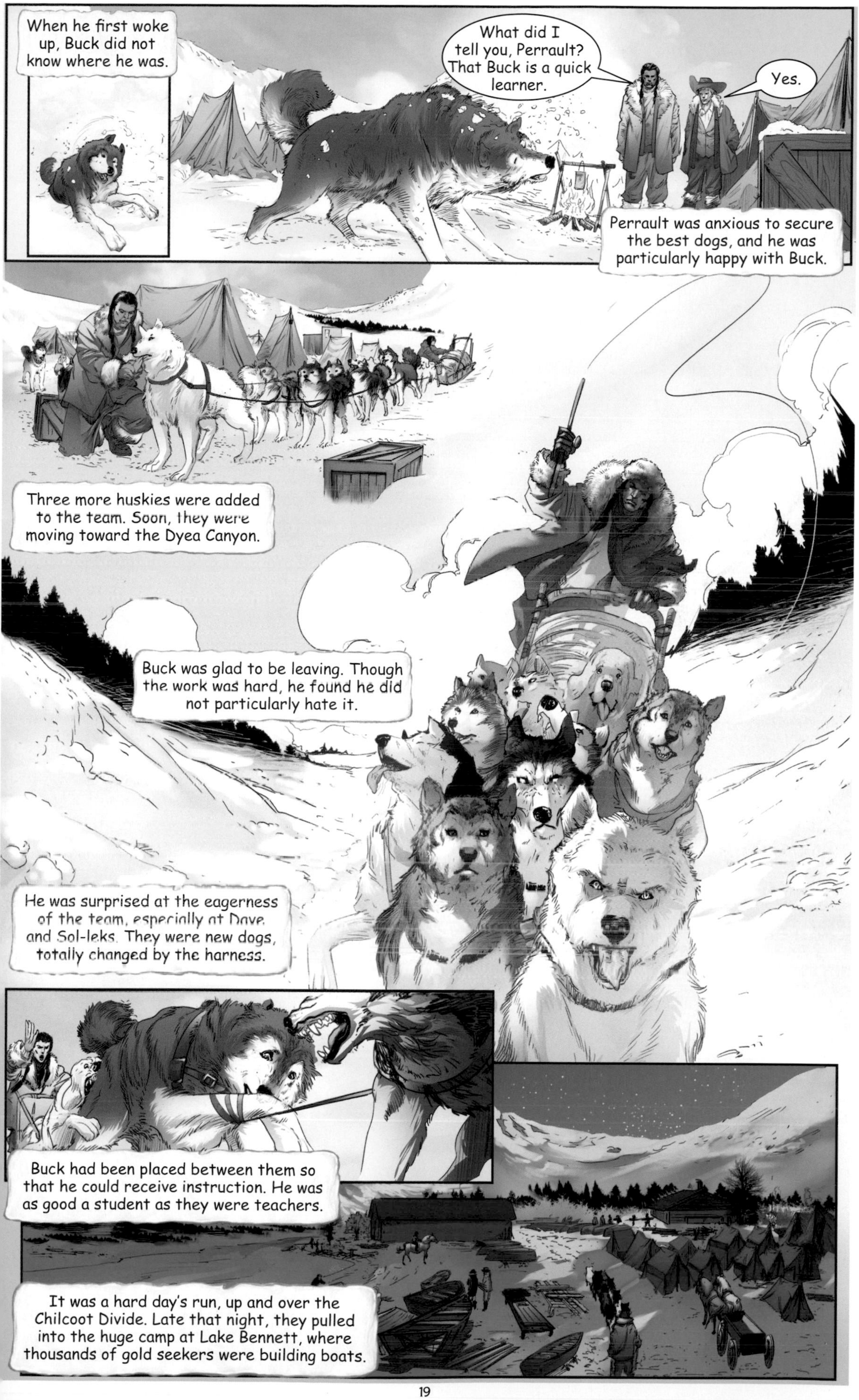
When he first woke up, Buck did not know where he was.
What did I tell you, Perrault? That Buck is a quick learner.
Yes.
Perrault was anxious to secure the best dogs, and he was particularly happy with Buck.
Three more huskies were added to the team. Soon, they were moving toward the Dyea Canyon.
Buck was glad to be leaving. Though the work was hard, he found he did not particularly hate it.
He was surprised at the eagerness of the team, especially at Dave and Sol-leks. They were new dogs, totally changed by the harness.
Buck had been placed between them so that he could receive instruction. He was as good a student as they were teachers.
It was a hard day's run, up and over the Chilcoot Divide. Late that night, they pulled into the huge camp at Lake Bennett, where thousands of gold seekers were building boats.

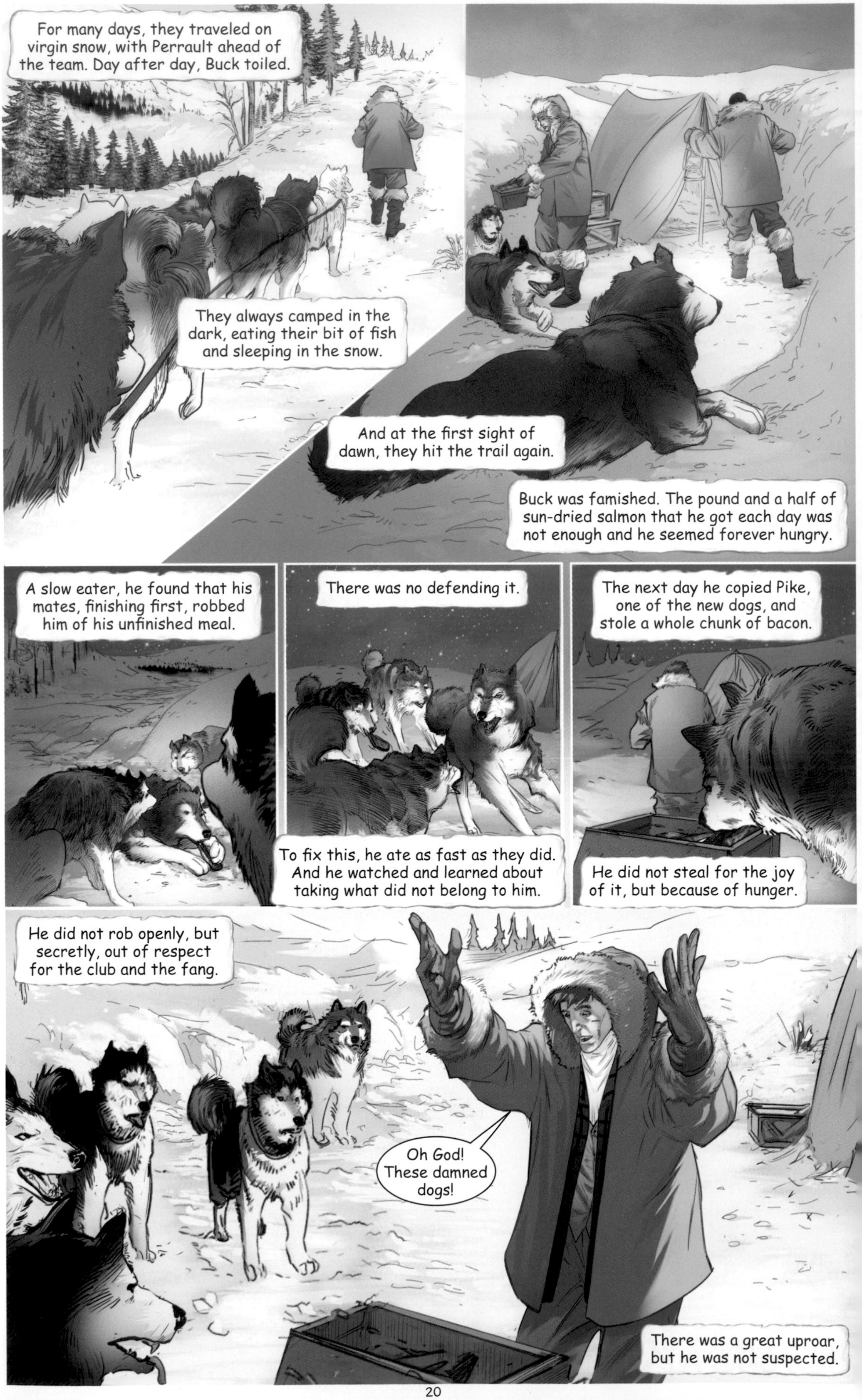
For many days, they traveled on virgin snow, with Perrault ahead of the team. Day after day, Buck toiled.
They always camped in the dark, eating their bit of fish and sleeping in the snow.
And at the first sight of dawn, they hit the trail again.
Buck was famished. The pound and a half of sun-dried salmon that he got each day was not enough and he seemed forever hungry.
A slow eater, he found that his mates, finishing first, robbed him of his unfinished meal.
There was no defending it.
To fix this, he ate as fast as they did. And he watched and learned about taking what did not belong to him.
The next day he copied Pike, one of the new dogs, and stole a whole chunk of bacon.
He did not steal for the joy of it, but because of hunger.
He did not rob openly, but secretly, out of respect for the club and the fang.
Oh God! These damned dogs!
There was a great uproar, but he was not suspected.

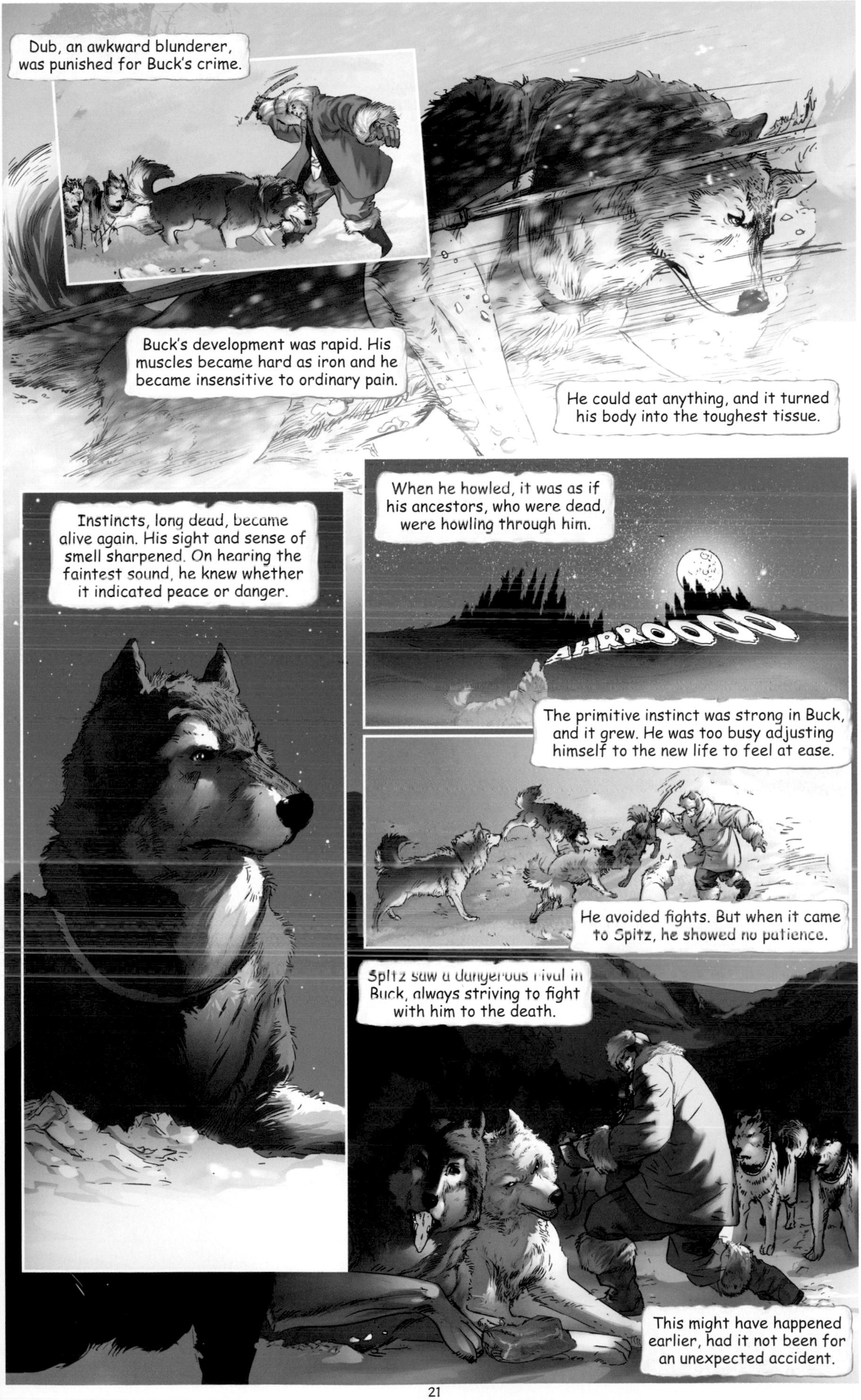
Dub, an awkward blunderer, was punished for Buck's crime.
Buck's development was rapid. His muscles became hard as iron and he became insensitive to ordinary pain.
He could eat anything, and it turned his body into the toughest tissue.
Instincts, long dead, became alive again. His sight and sense of smell sharpened. On hearing the faintest sound, he knew whether it indicated peace or danger.
When he howled, it was as if his ancestors, who were dead, were howling through him.
AHRROOOO
The primitive instinct was strong in Buck, and it grew. He was too busy adjusting himself to the new life to feel at ease.
He avoided fights. But when it came to Spitz, he showed no patience.
Spitz saw a dangerous rival in Buck, always striving to fight with him to the death.
This might have happened earlier, had it not been for an unexpected accident.

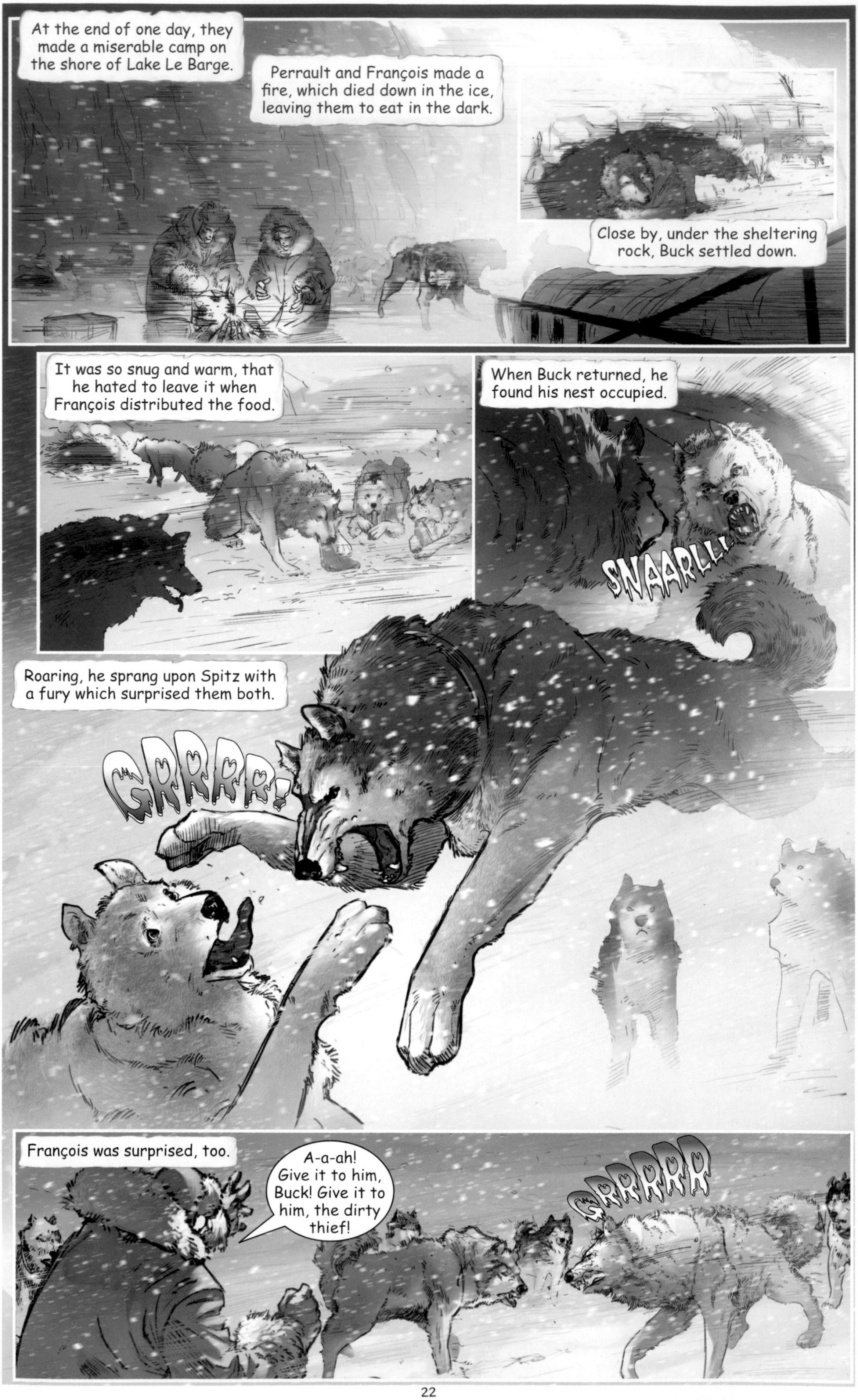
At the end of one day, they made a miserable camp on the shore of Lake Le Barge.
Perrault and François made a fire, which died down in the ice, leaving them to eat in the dark.
Close by, under the sheltering rock, Buck settled down.
It was so snug and warm, that he hated to leave it when François distributed the food.
When Buck returned, he found his nest occupied.
SNAARLLL
Roaring, he sprang upon Spitz with a fury which surprised them both.
GRRRR!
François was surprised, too.
A-a-ah! Give it to him, Buck! Give it to him, the dirty thief!
GRRRRR

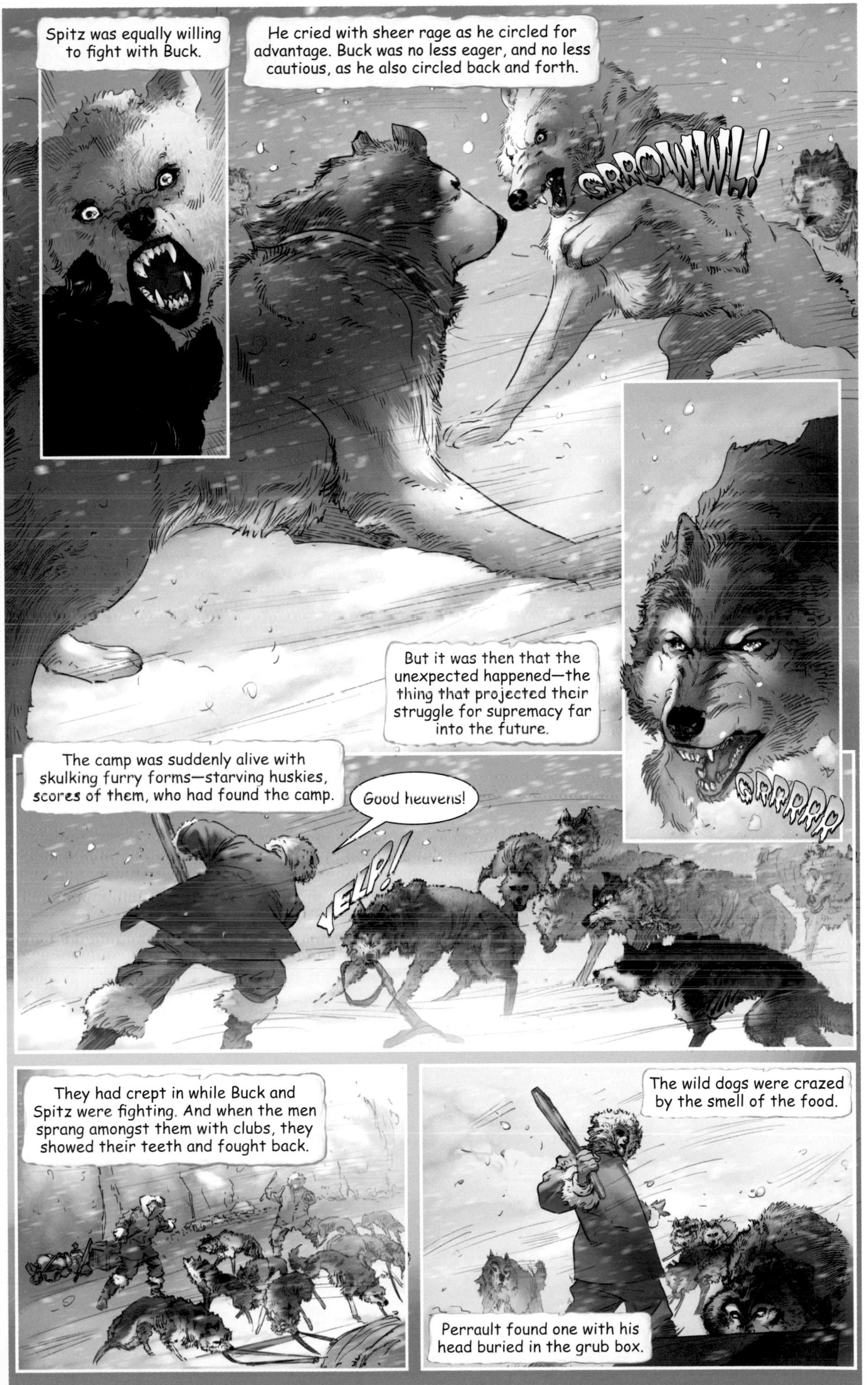
Spitz was equally willing to fight with Buck.
He cried with sheer rage as he circled for advantage. Buck was no less eager, and no less cautious, as he also circled back and forth.
GRROWWL!
But it was then that the unexpected happened—the thing that projected their struggle for supremacy far into the future.
GRRRRR
The camp was suddenly alive with skulking furry forms—starving huskies, scores of them, who had found the camp.
Good heavens!
YELP!
They had crept in while Buck and Spitz were fighting. And when the men sprang amongst them with clubs, they showed their teeth and fought back.
The wild dogs were crazed by the smell of the food.
Perrault found one with his head buried in the grub box.

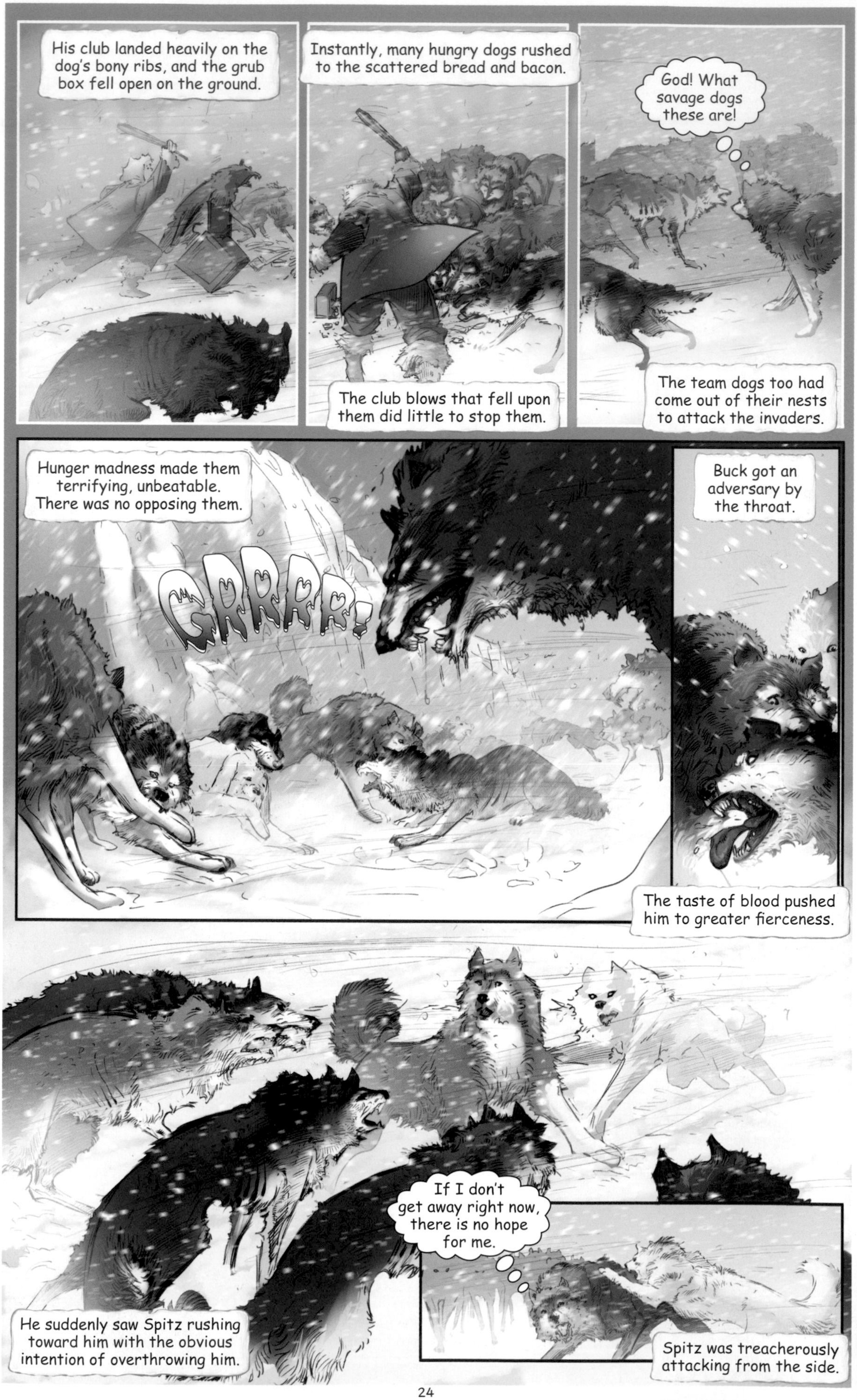
His club landed heavily on the dog's bony ribs, and the grub box fell open on the ground.
Instantly, many hungry dogs rushed to the scattered bread and bacon.
The club blows that fell upon them did little to stop them.
God! What savage dogs these are!
The team dogs too had come out of their nests to attack the invaders.
Hunger madness made them terrifying, unbeatable. There was no opposing them.
GRRRR!
Buck got an adversary by the throat.
The taste of blood pushed him to greater fierceness.
He suddenly saw Spitz rushing toward him with the obvious intention of overthrowing him.
If I don't get away right now, there is no hope for me.
Spitz was treacherously attacking from the side.

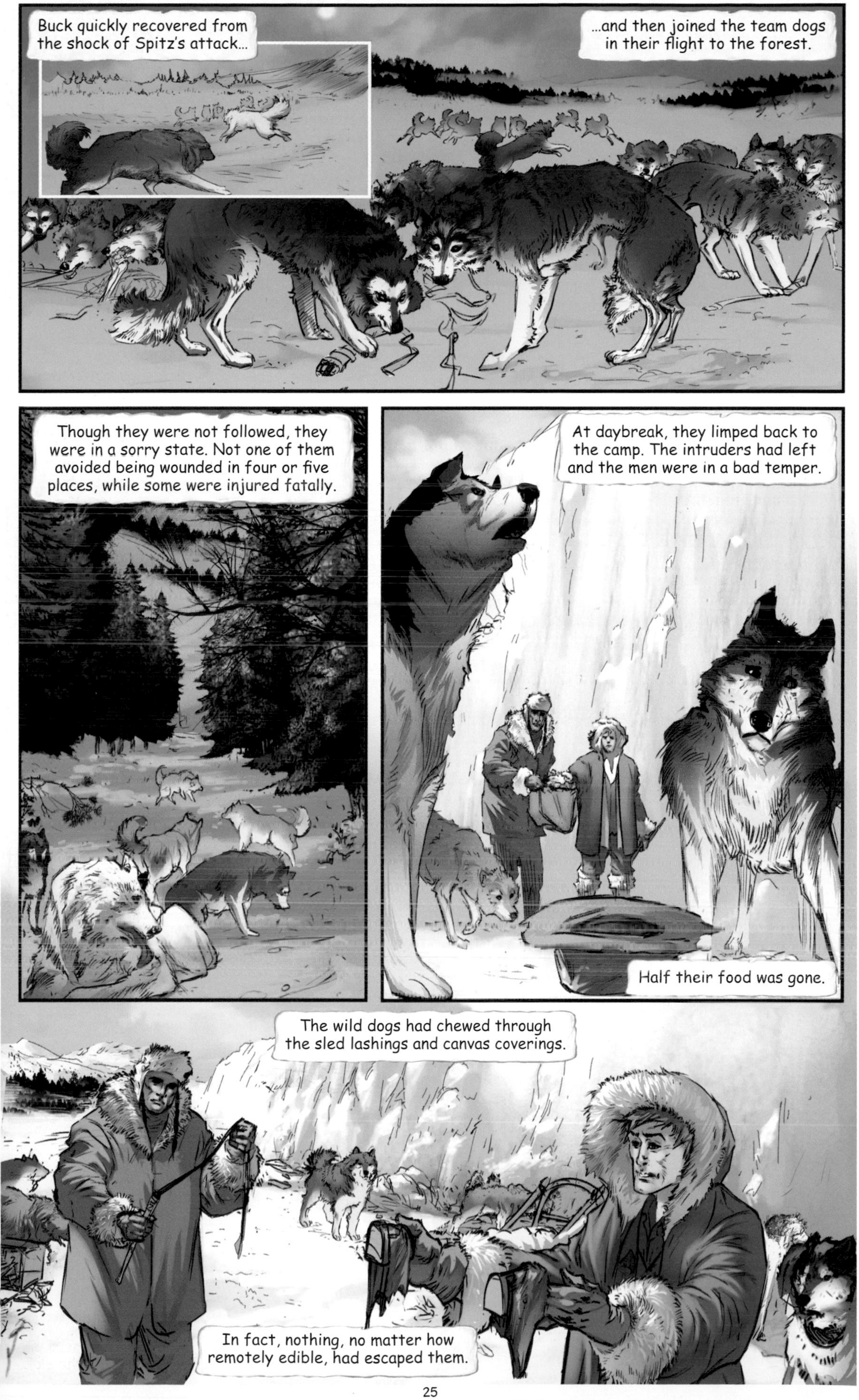
Buck quickly recovered from the shock of Spitz's attack...
...and then joined the team dogs in their flight to the forest.
Though they were not followed, they were in a sorry state. Not one of them avoided being wounded in four or five places, while some were injured fatally.
At daybreak, they limped back to the camp. The intruders had left and the men were in a bad temper.
Half their food was gone.
The wild dogs had chewed through the sled lashings and canvas coverings.
In fact, nothing, no matter how remotely edible, had escaped them.

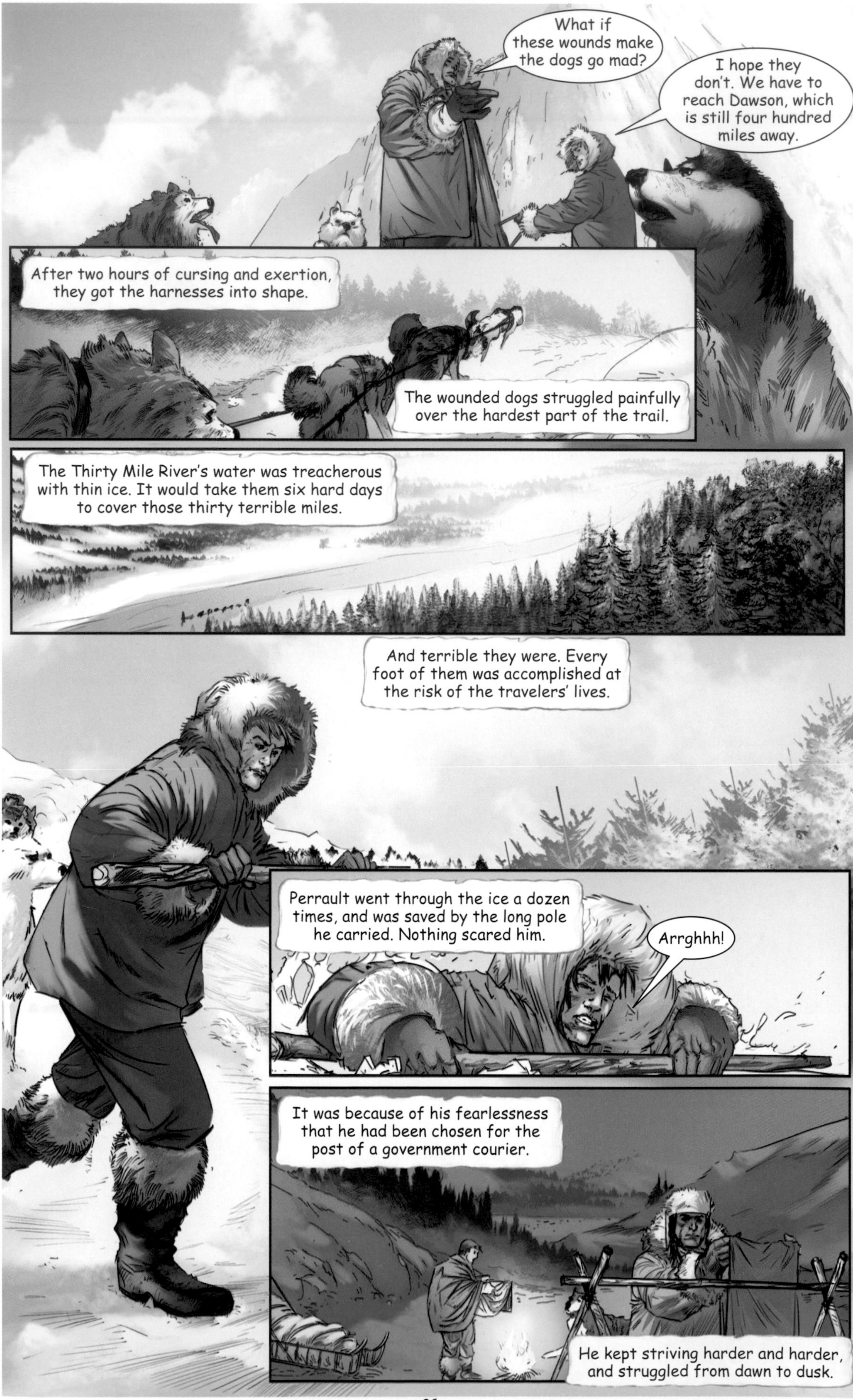

What if these wounds make the dogs go mad?
I hope they don't. We have to reach Dawson, which is still four hundred miles away.
After two hours of cursing and exertion, they got the harnesses into shape.
The wounded dogs struggled painfully over the hardest part of the trail.
The Thirty Mile River's water was treacherous with thin ice. It would take them six hard days to cover those thirty terrible miles.
And terrible they were. Every foot of them was accomplished at the risk of the travelers' lives.
Perrault went through the ice a dozen times, and was saved by the long pole he carried. Nothing scared him.
Arrghhh!
It was because of his fearlessness that he had been chosen for the post of a government courier.
He kept striving harder and harder, and struggled from dawn to dusk.

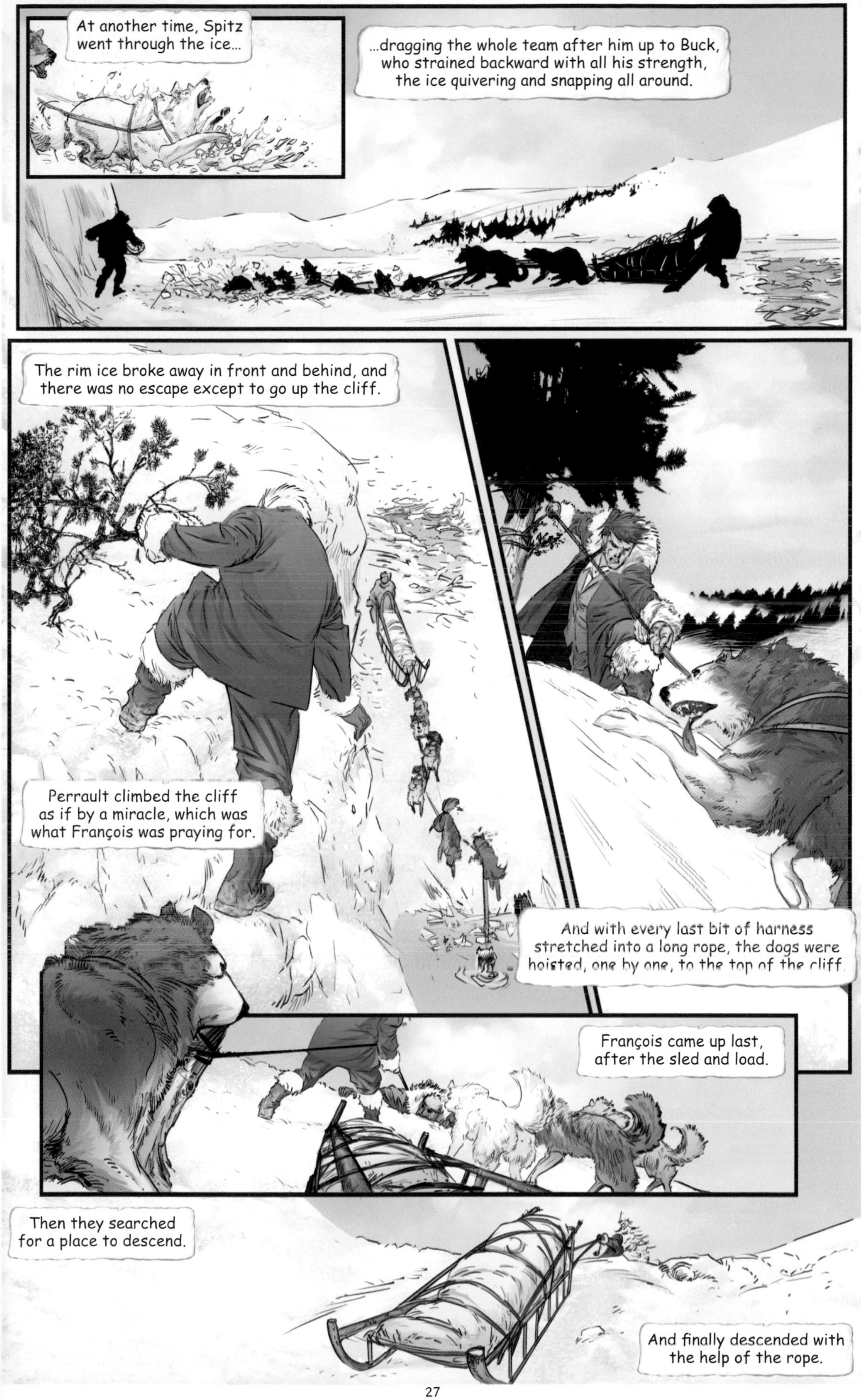
At another time, Spitz went through the ice...
...dragging the whole team after him up to Buck, who strained backward with all his strength, the ice quivering and snapping all around.
The rim ice broke away in front and behind, and there was no escape except to go up the cliff.
Perrault climbed the cliff as if by a miracle, which was what François was praying for.
And with every last bit of harness stretched into a long rope, the dogs were hoisted, one by one, to the top of the cliff.
François came up last, after the sled and load.
Then they searched for a place to descend.
And finally descended with the help of the rope.

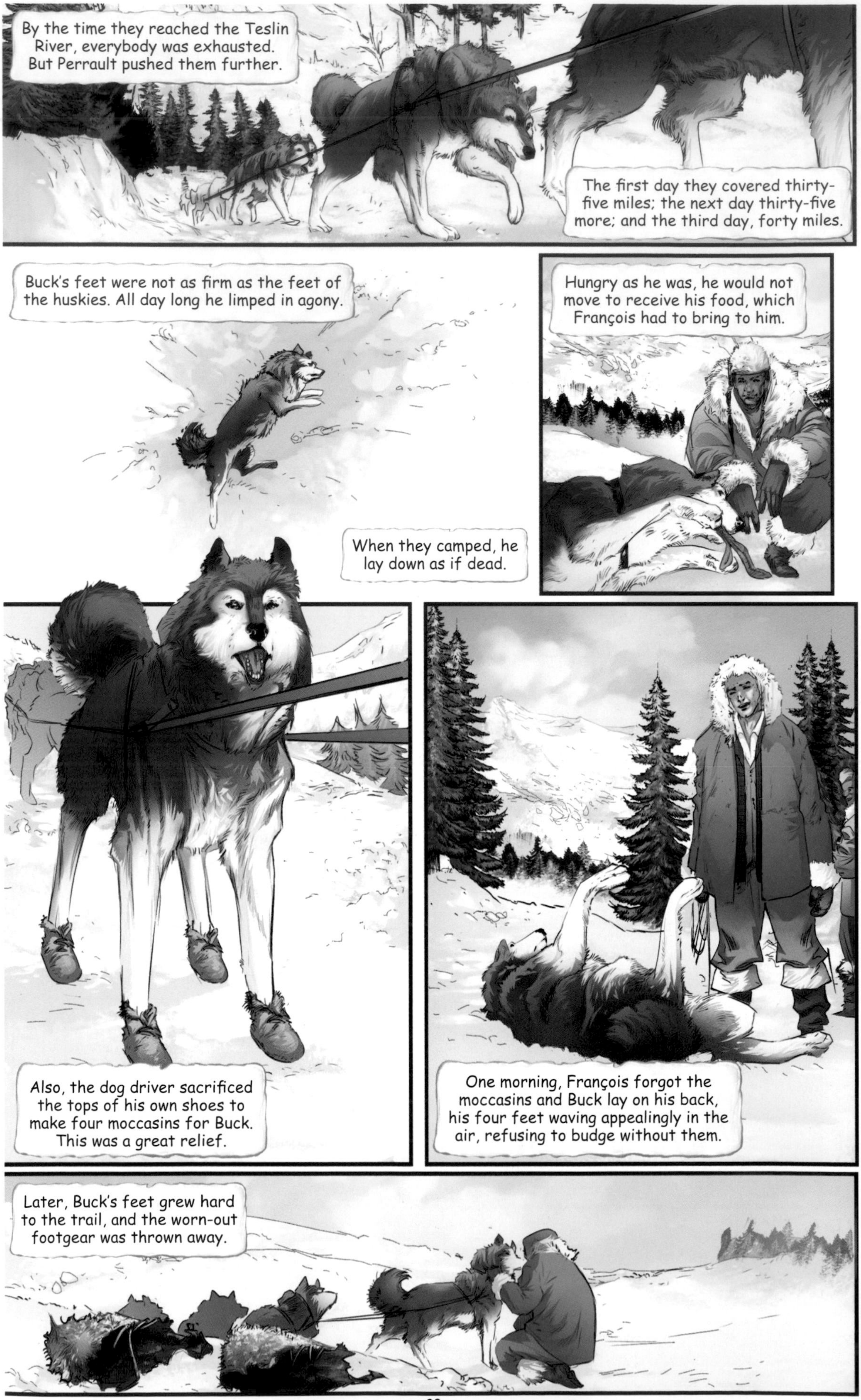
By the time they reached the Teslin River, everybody was exhausted. But Perrault pushed them further.
The first day they covered thirty-five miles; the next day thirty-five more; and the third day, forty miles.
Buck's feet were not as firm as the feet of the huskies. All day long he limped in agony.
When they camped, he lay down as if dead.
Hungry as he was, he would not move to receive his food, which François had to bring to him.
Also, the dog driver sacrificed the tops of his own shoes to make four moccasins for Buck. This was a great relief.
One morning, François forgot the moccasins and Buck lay on his back, his four feet waving appealingly in the air, refusing to budge without them.
Later, Buck's feet grew hard to the trail, and the worn-out footgear was thrown away.

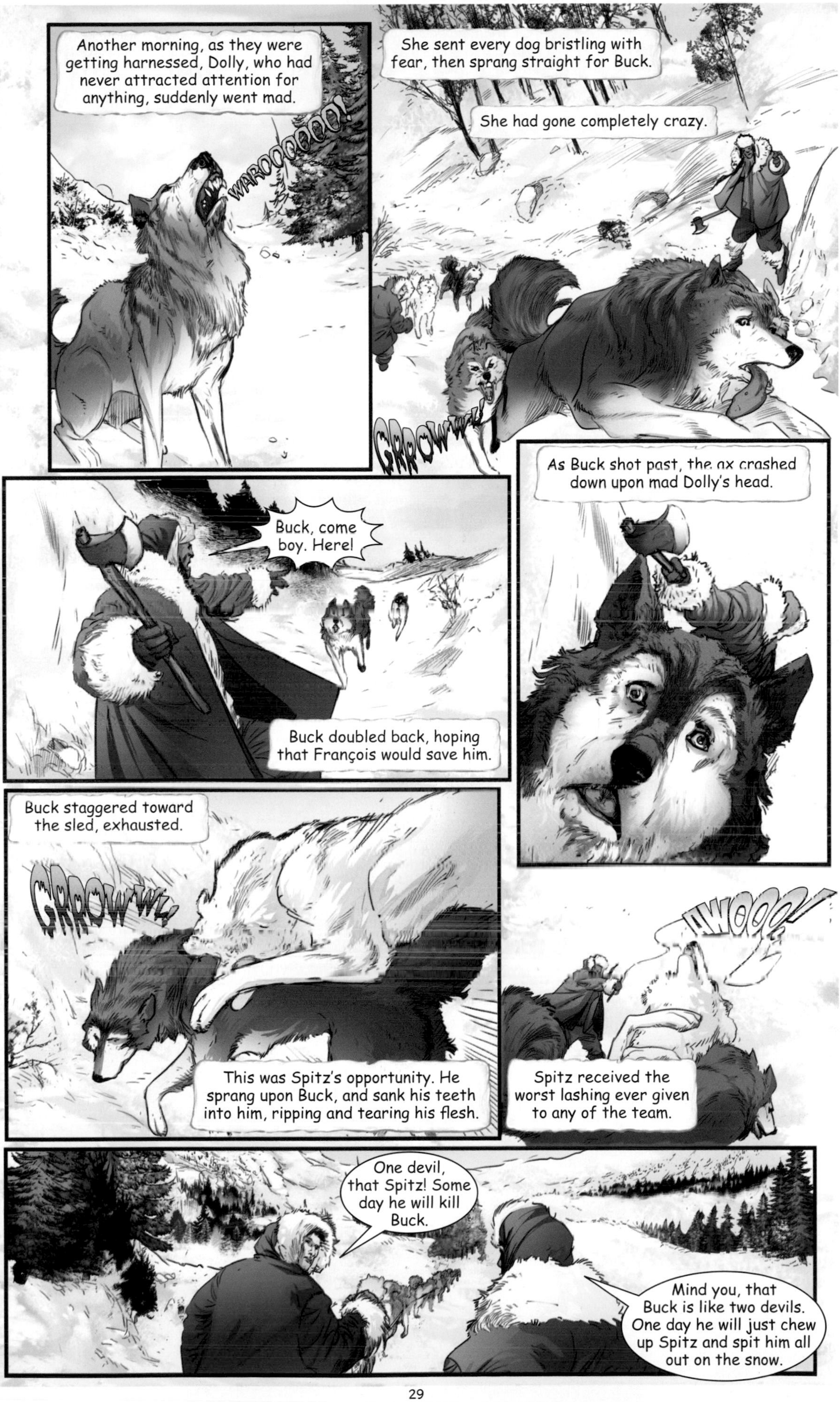
Another morning, as they were getting harnessed, Dolly, who had never attracted attention for anything, suddenly went mad.
WAROOOOOOOO!
She sent every dog bristling with fear, then sprang straight for Buck.
She had gone completely crazy.
GRROWWL!
Buck, come boy. Here!
Buck doubled back, hoping that François would save him.
As Buck shot past, the ax crashed down upon mad Dolly's head.
Buck staggered toward the sled, exhausted.
GRROWWL!
This was Spitz's opportunity. He sprang upon Buck, and sank his teeth into him, ripping and tearing his flesh.
AWOOO!
Spitz received the worst lashing ever given to any of the team.
One devil, that Spitz! Some day he will kill Buck.
Mind you, that Buck is like two devils. One day he will just chew up Spitz and spit him all out on the snow.

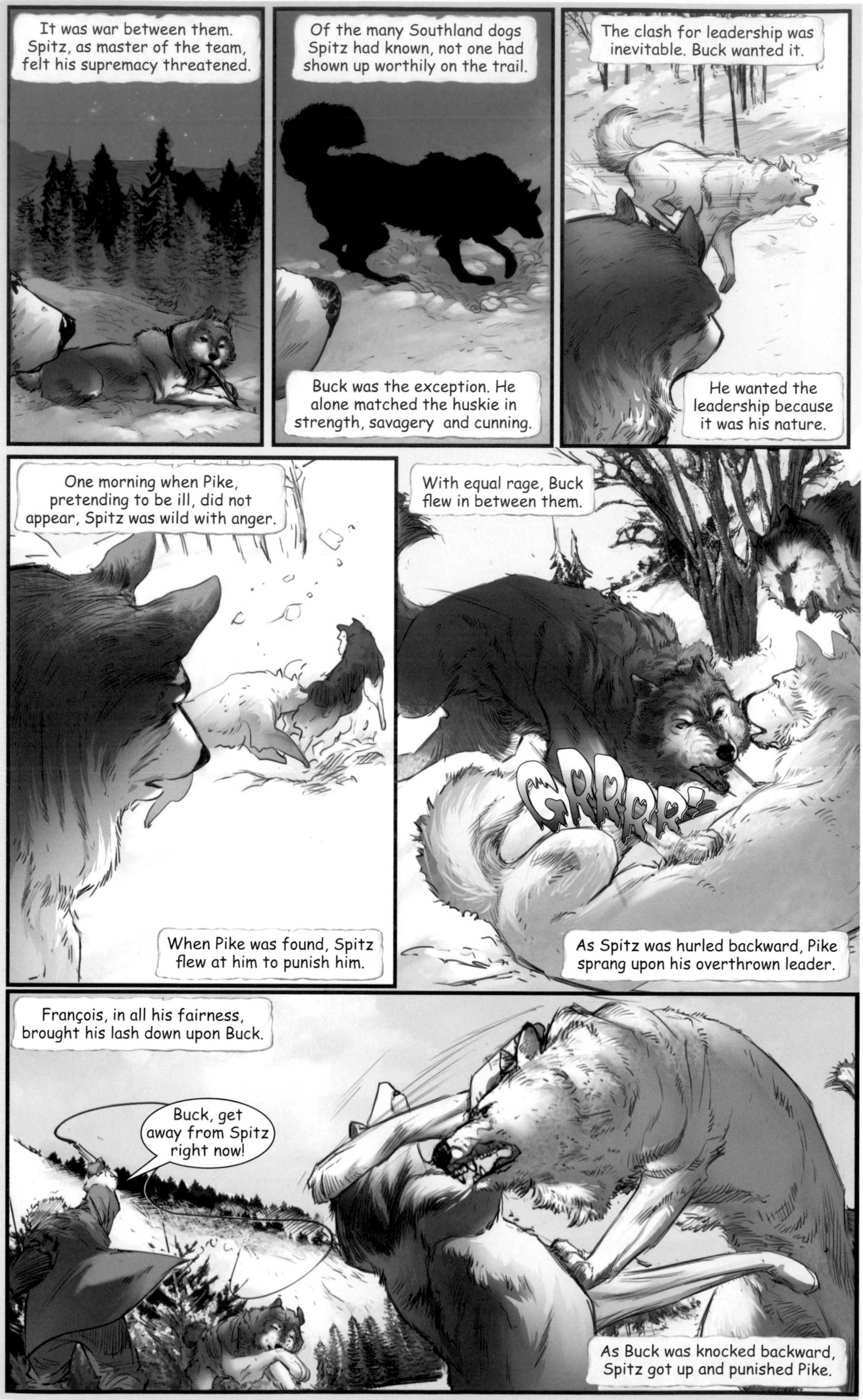
It was war between them. Spitz, as master of the team, felt his supremacy threatened.
Of the many Southland dogs Spitz had known, not one had shown up worthily on the trail.
Buck was the exception. He alone matched the huskie in strength, savagery and cunning.
The clash for leadership was inevitable. Buck wanted it.
He wanted the leadership because it was his nature.
One morning when Pike, pretending to be ill, did not appear, Spitz was wild with anger.
When Pike was found, Spitz flew at him to punish him.
With equal rage, Buck flew in between them.
GRRRR!
As Spitz was hurled backward, Pike sprang upon his overthrown leader.
François, in all his fairness, brought his lash down upon Buck.
Buck, get away from Spitz right now!
As Buck was knocked backward, Spitz got up and punished Pike.

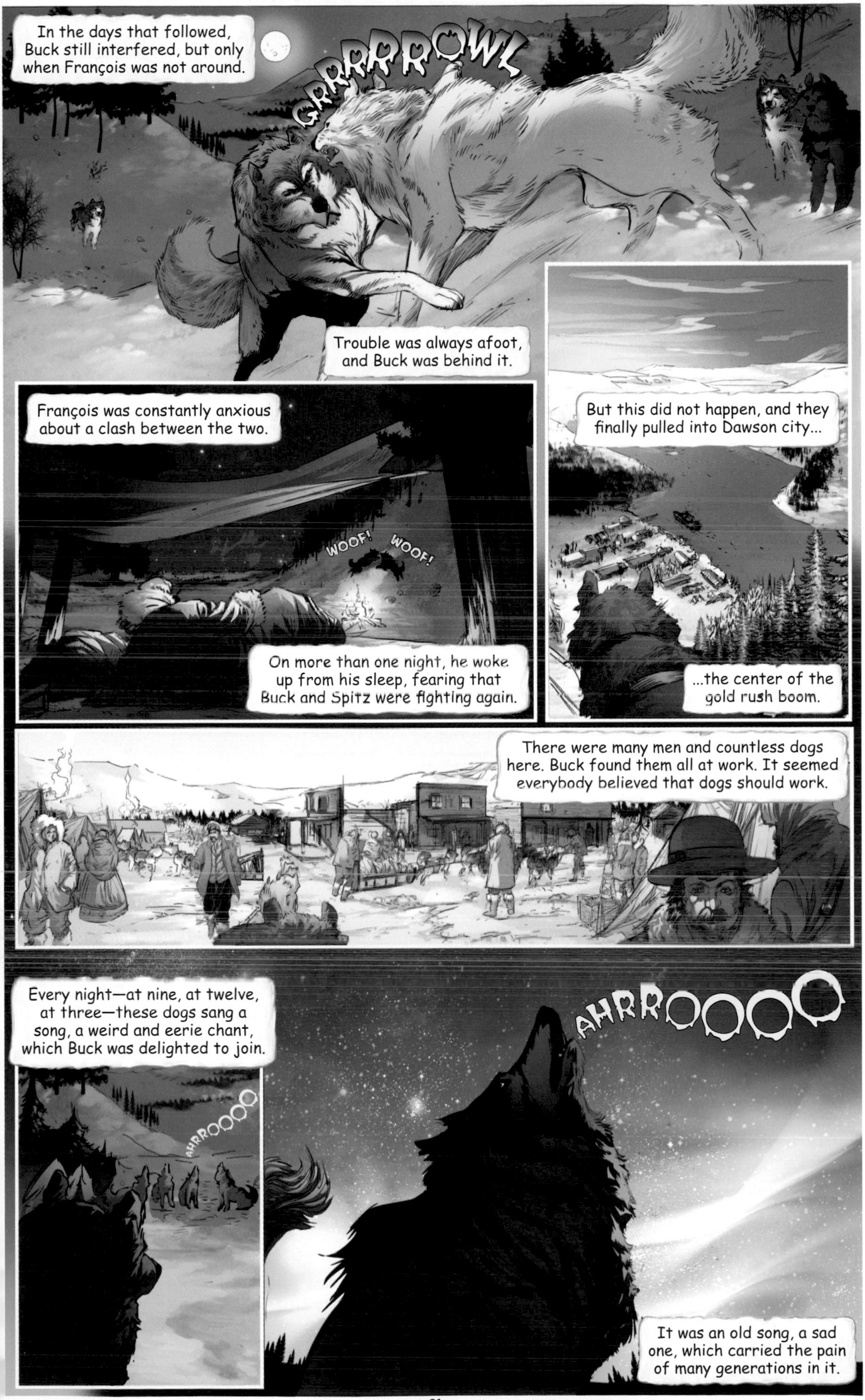
In the days that followed, Buck still interfered, but only when François was not around.
GRRRRROWL
Trouble was always afoot, and Buck was behind it.
François was constantly anxious about a clash between the two.
WOOF! WOOF!
On more than one night, he woke up from his sleep, fearing that Buck and Spitz were fighting again.
But this did not happen, and they finally pulled into Dawson city...
...the center of the gold rush boom.
There were many men and countless dogs here. Buck found them all at work. It seemed everybody believed that dogs should work.
Every night—at nine, at twelve, at three—these dogs sang a song, a weird and eerie chant, which Buck was delighted to join.
AHRROOOO
AHRROOOO
It was an old song, a sad one, which carried the pain of many generations in it.

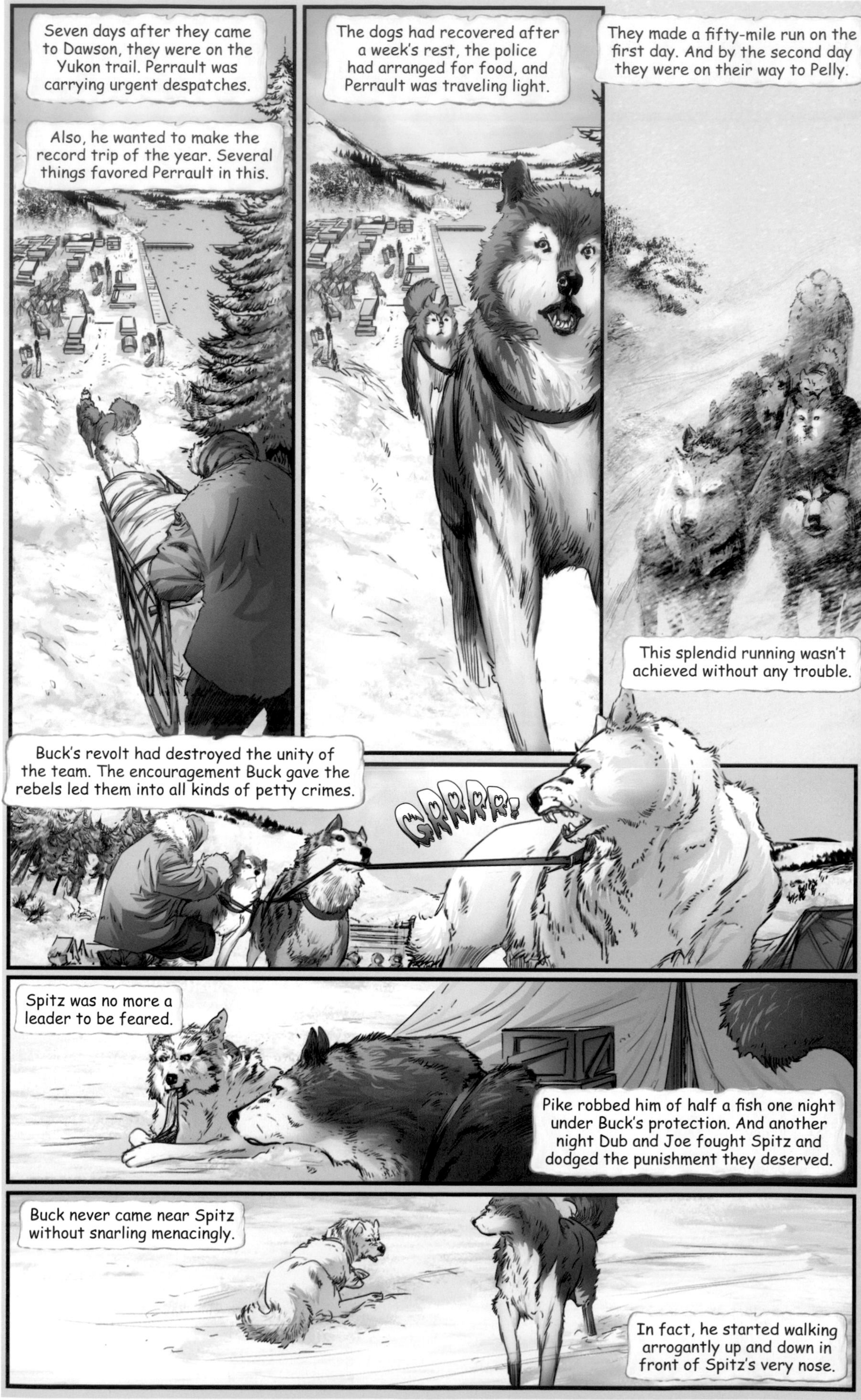

Seven days after they came to Dawson, they were on the Yukon trail. Perrault was carrying urgent despatches.
Also, he wanted to make the record trip of the year. Several things favored Perrault in this.
The dogs had recovered after a week's rest, the police had arranged for food, and Perrault was traveling light.
They made a fifty-mile run on the first day. And by the second day they were on their way to Pelly.
This splendid running wasn't achieved without any trouble.
Buck's revolt had destroyed the unity of the team. The encouragement Buck gave the rebels led them into all kinds of petty crimes.
GRRRR!
Spitz was no more a leader to be feared.
Pike robbed him of half a fish one night under Buck's protection. And another night Dub and Joe fought Spitz and dodged the punishment they deserved.
Buck never came near Spitz without snarling menacingly.
In fact, he started walking arrogantly up and down in front of Spitz's very nose.

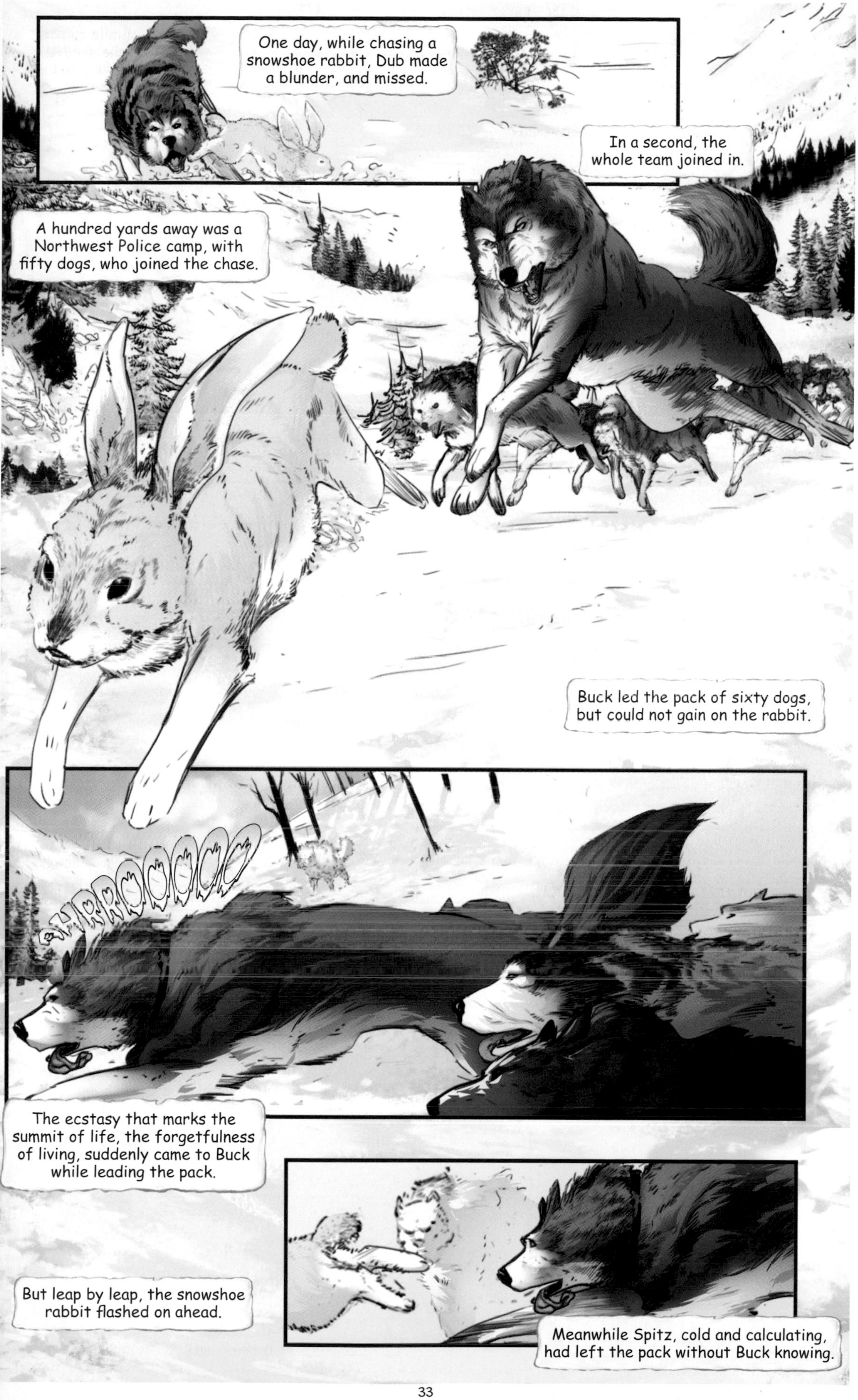
One day, while chasing a snowshoe rabbit, Dub made a blunder, and missed.
In a second, the whole team joined in.
A hundred yards away was a Northwest Police camp, with fifty dogs, who joined the chase.
Buck led the pack of sixty dogs, but could not gain on the rabbit.
WHROOOOOO
The ecstasy that marks the summit of life, the forgetfulness of living, suddenly came to Buck while leading the pack.
But leap by leap, the snowshoe rabbit flashed on ahead.
Meanwhile Spitz, cold and calculating, had left the pack without Buck knowing.

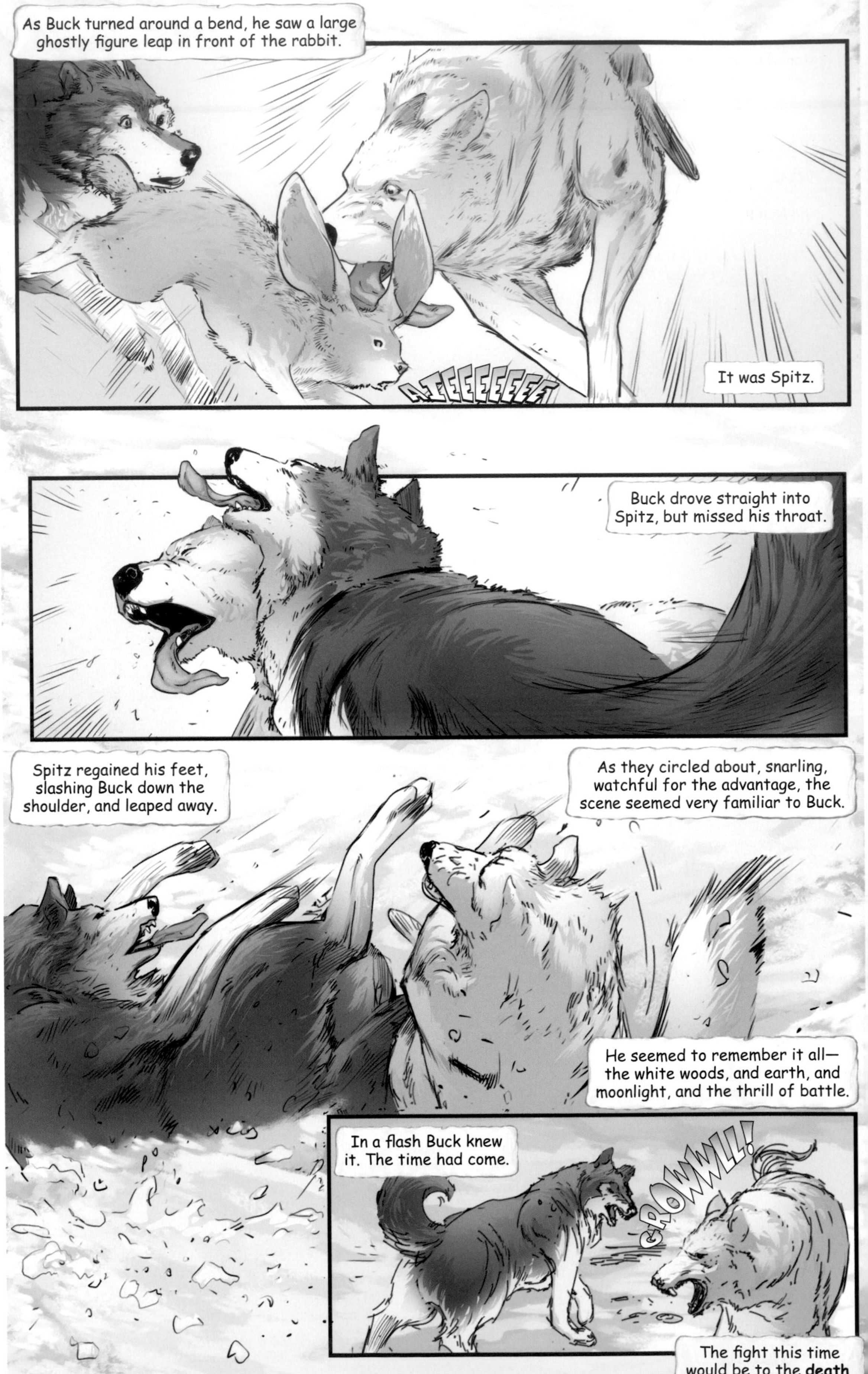
As Buck turned around a bend, he saw a large ghostly figure leap in front of the rabbit.
AIEEEEEEE
It was Spitz.
Buck drove straight into Spitz, but missed his throat.
Spitz regained his feet, slashing Buck down the shoulder, and leaped away.
As they circled about, snarling, watchful for the advantage, the scene seemed very familiar to Buck.
He seemed to remember it all— the white woods, and earth, and moonlight, and the thrill of battle.
In a flash Buck knew it. The time had come.
GROWWLL!
The fight this time would be to the **death**.

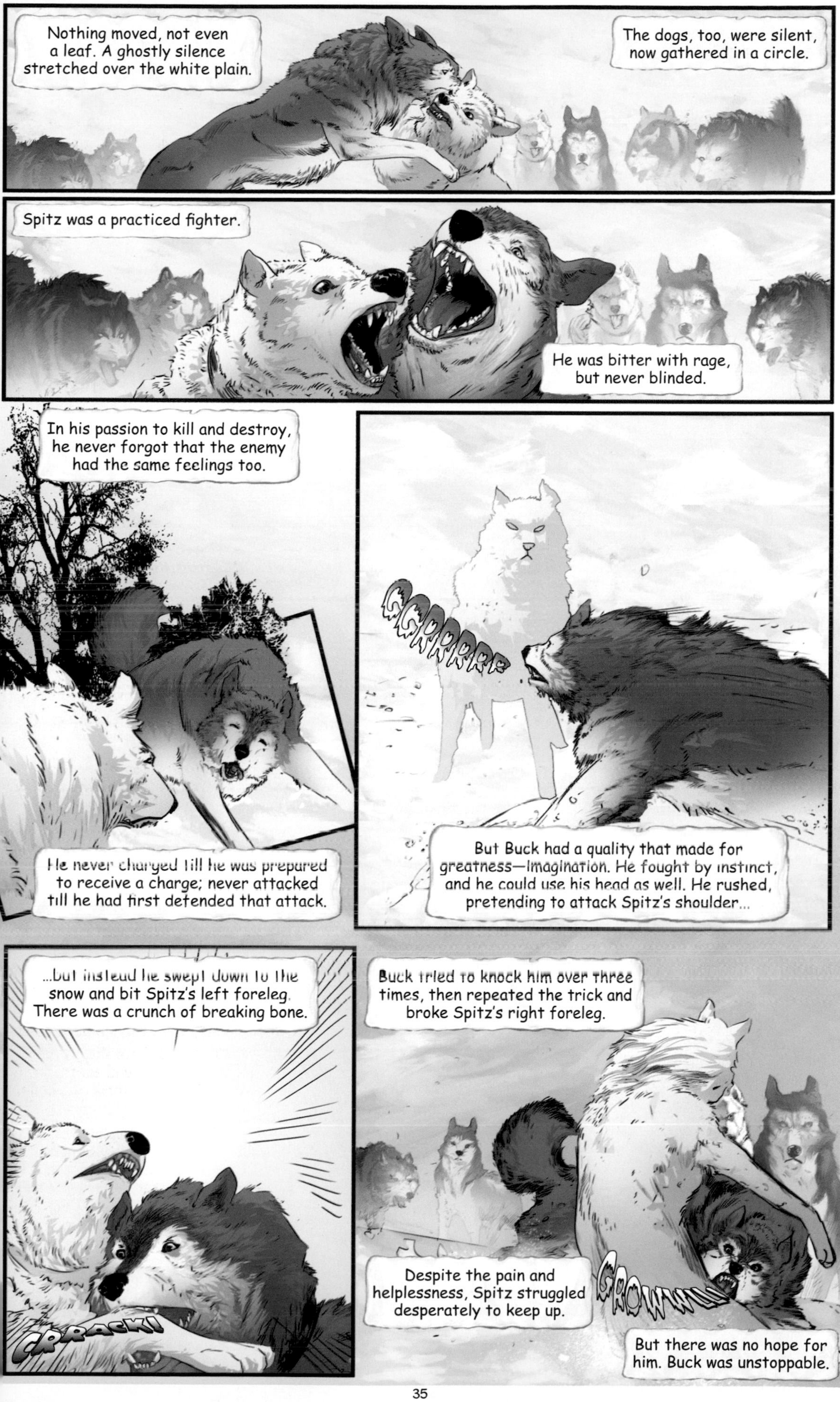
Nothing moved, not even a leaf. A ghostly silence stretched over the white plain.
The dogs, too, were silent, now gathered in a circle.
Spitz was a practiced fighter.
He was bitter with rage, but never blinded.
In his passion to kill and destroy, he never forgot that the enemy had the same feelings too.
He never charged till he was prepared to receive a charge; never attacked till he had first defended that attack.
But Buck had a quality that made for greatness—Imagination. He fought by instinct, and he could use his head as well. He rushed, pretending to attack Spitz's shoulder...
...but instead he swept down to the snow and bit Spitz's left foreleg. There was a crunch of breaking bone.
Buck tried to knock him over three times, then repeated the trick and broke Spitz's right foreleg.
Despite the pain and helplessness, Spitz struggled desperately to keep up.
But there was no hope for him. Buck was unstoppable.

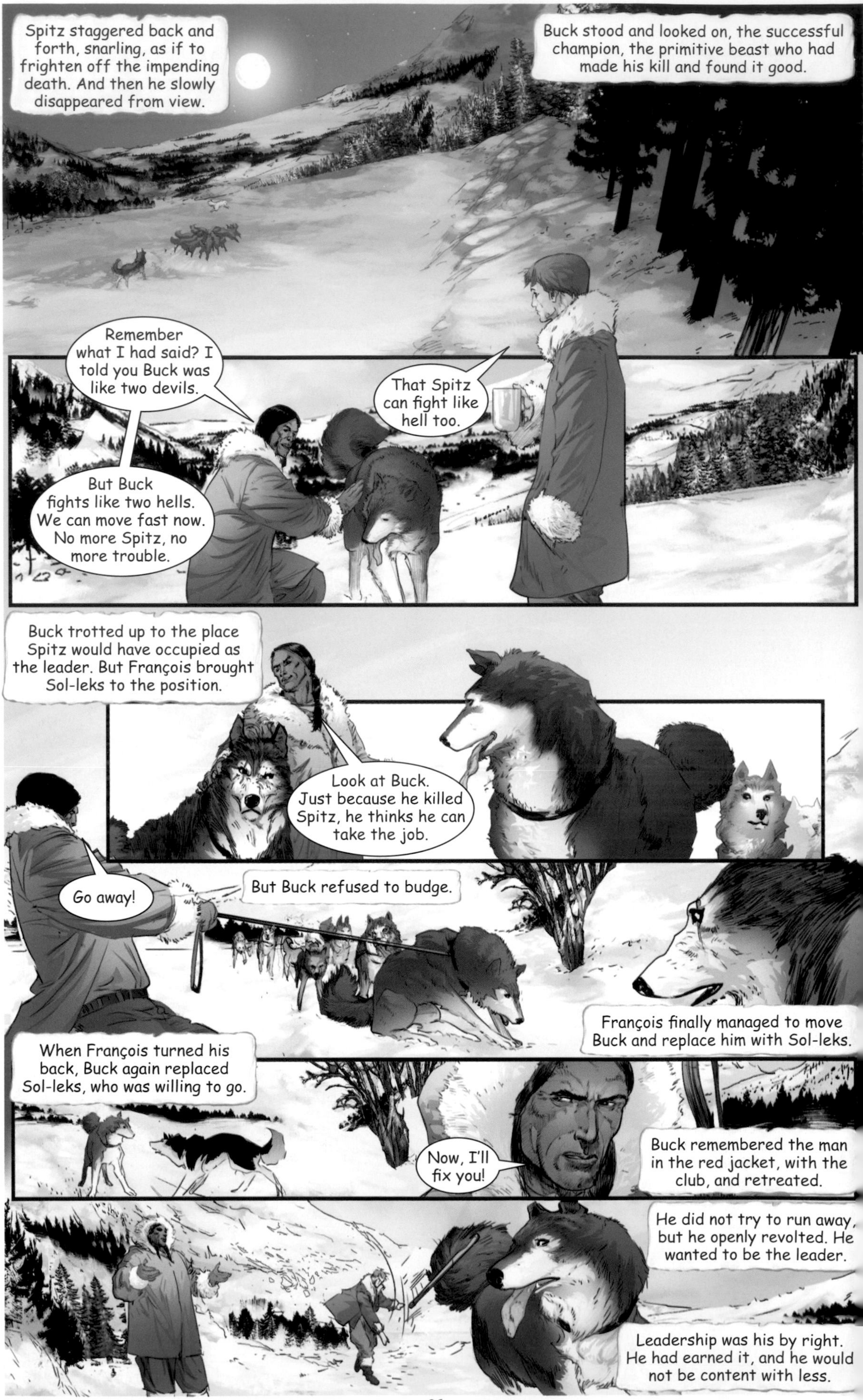
Spitz staggered back and forth, snarling, as if to frighten off the impending death. And then he slowly disappeared from view.
Buck stood and looked on, the successful champion, the primitive beast who had made his kill and found it good.
Remember what I had said? I told you Buck was like two devils.
That Spitz can fight like hell too.
But Buck fights like two hells. We can move fast now. No more Spitz, no more trouble.
Buck trotted up to the place Spitz would have occupied as the leader. But François brought Sol-leks to the position.
Look at Buck. Just because he killed Spitz, he thinks he can take the job.
Go away!
But Buck refused to budge.
François finally managed to move Buck and replace him with Sol-leks.
When François turned his back, Buck again replaced Sol-leks, who was willing to go.
Now, I'll fix you!
Buck remembered the man in the red jacket, with the club, and retreated.
He did not try to run away, but he openly revolted. He wanted to be the leader.
Leadership was his by right. He had earned it, and he would not be content with less.

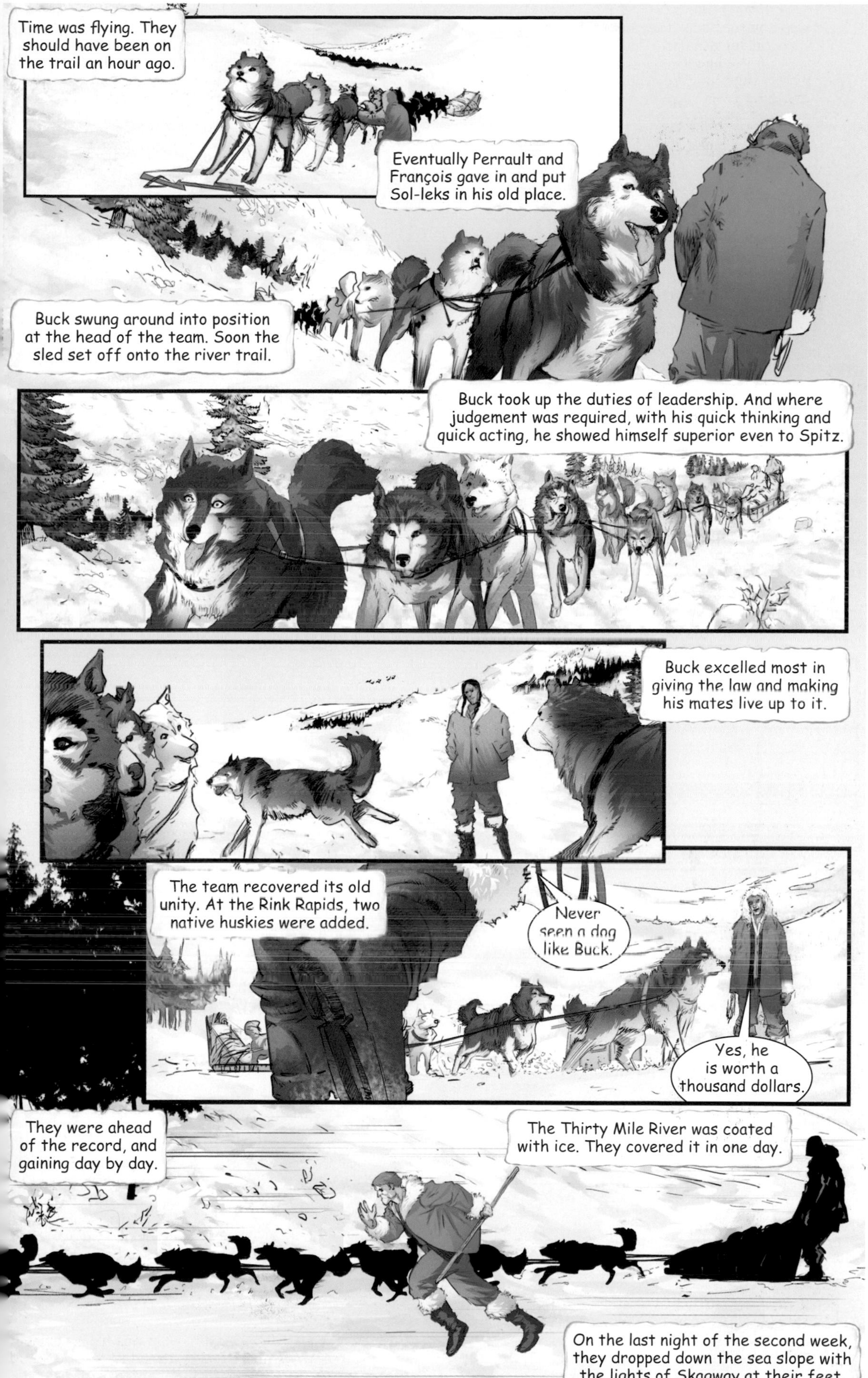
Time was flying. They should have been on the trail an hour ago.
Eventually Perrault and François gave in and put Sol-leks in his old place.
Buck swung around into position at the head of the team. Soon the sled set off onto the river trail.
Buck took up the duties of leadership. And where judgement was required, with his quick thinking and quick acting, he showed himself superior even to Spitz.
Buck excelled most in giving the law and making his mates live up to it.
The team recovered its old unity. At the Rink Rapids, two native huskies were added.
Never seen a dog like Buck.
Yes, he is worth a thousand dollars.
They were ahead of the record, and gaining day by day.
The Thirty Mile River was coated with ice. They covered it in one day.
On the last night of the second week, they dropped down the sea slope with the lights of Skagway at their feet.

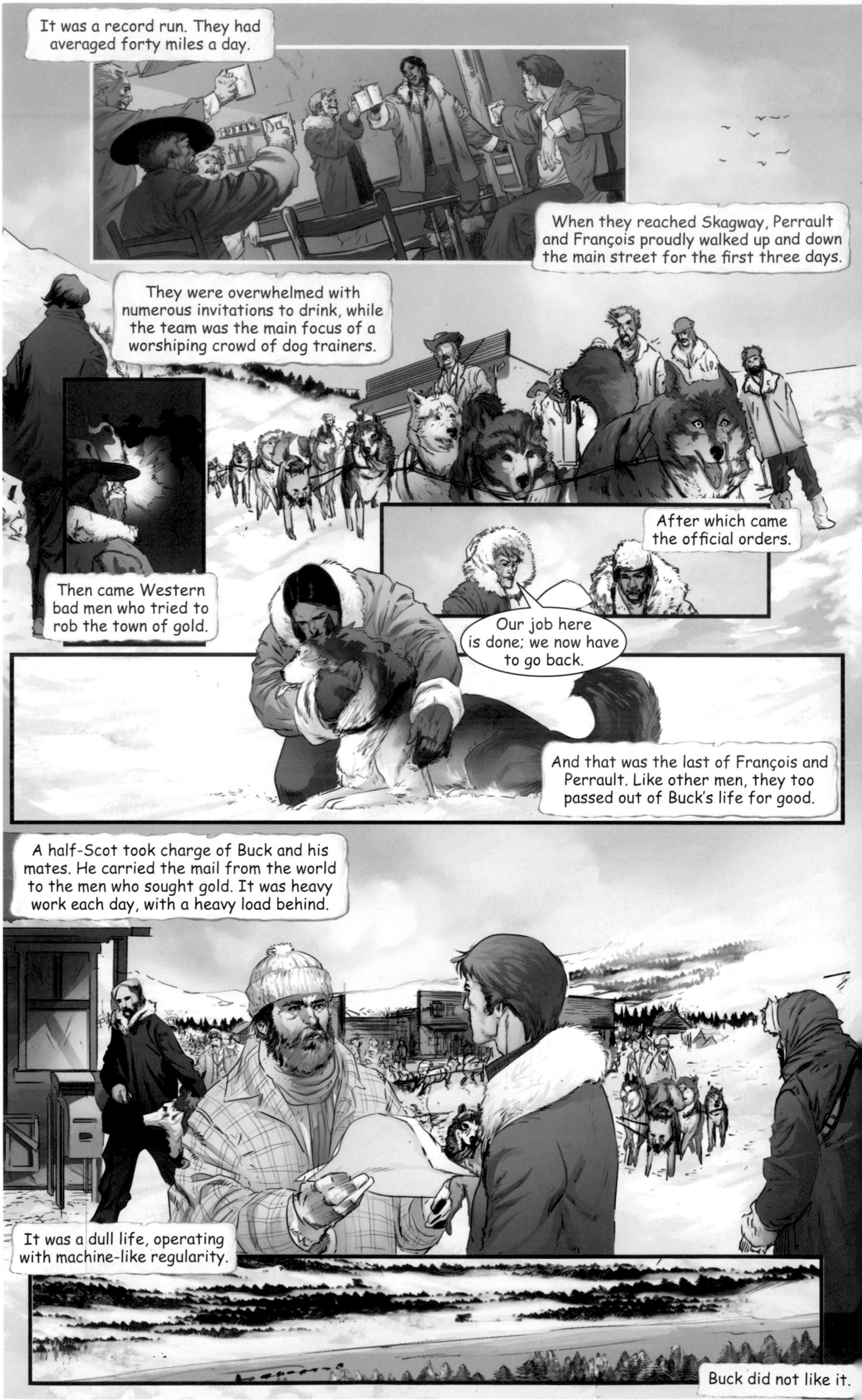
It was a record run. They had averaged forty miles a day.
When they reached Skagway, Perrault and François proudly walked up and down the main street for the first three days.
They were overwhelmed with numerous invitations to drink, while the team was the main focus of a worshiping crowd of dog trainers.
Then came Western bad men who tried to rob the town of gold.
After which came the official orders.
Our job here is done; we now have to go back.
And that was the last of François and Perrault. Like other men, they too passed out of Buck's life for good.
A half-Scot took charge of Buck and his mates. He carried the mail from the world to the men who sought gold. It was heavy work each day, with a heavy load behind.
It was a dull life, operating with machine-like regularity.
Buck did not like it.

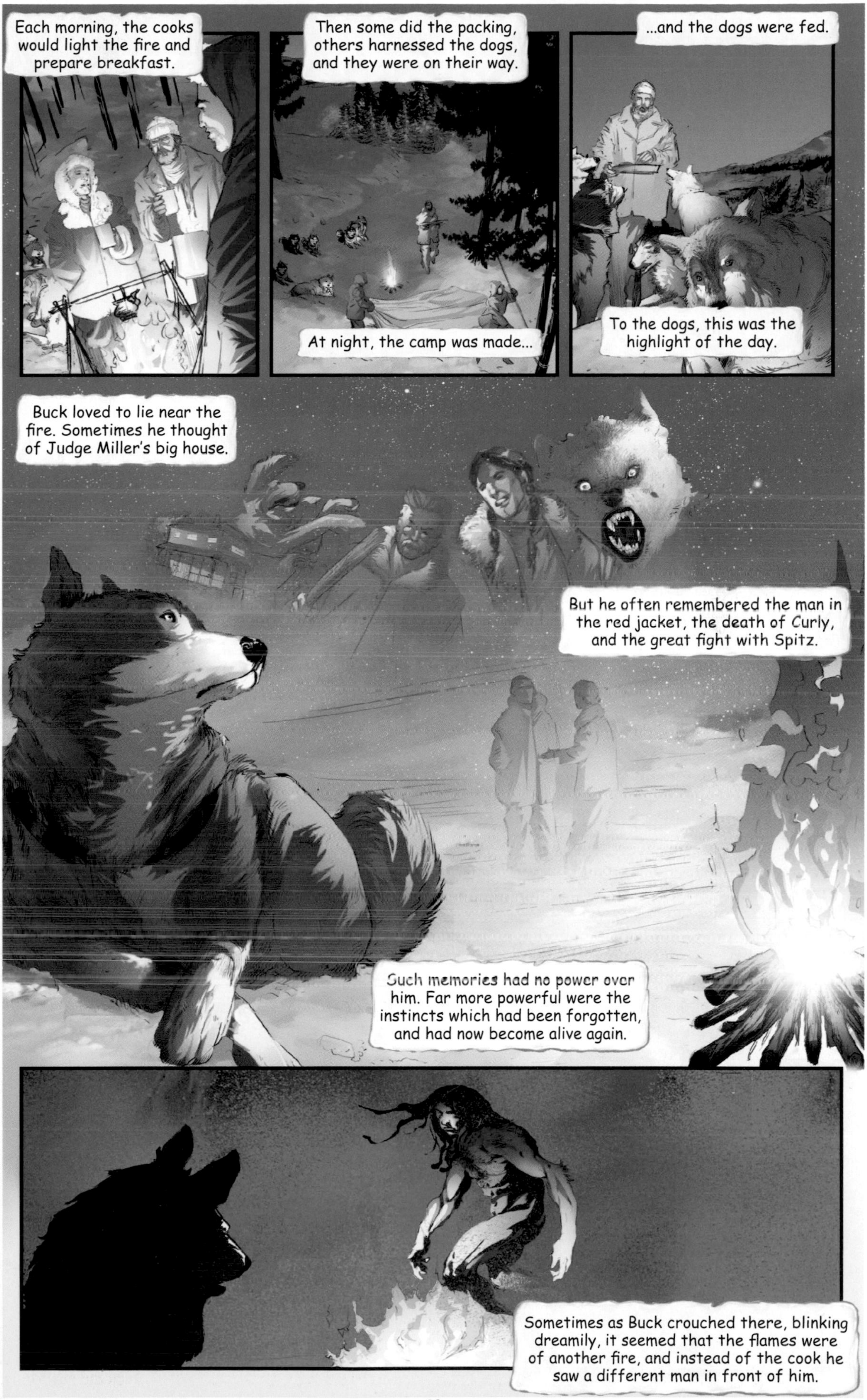
Each morning, the cooks would light the fire and prepare breakfast.
Then some did the packing, others harnessed the dogs, and they were on their way.
At night, the camp was made...
...and the dogs were fed.
To the dogs, this was the highlight of the day.
Buck loved to lie near the fire. Sometimes he thought of Judge Miller's big house.
But he often remembered the man in the red jacket, the death of Curly, and the great fight with Spitz.
Such memories had no power over him. Far more powerful were the instincts which had been forgotten, and had now become alive again.
Sometimes as Buck crouched there, blinking dreamily, it seemed that the flames were of another fire, and instead of the cook he saw a different man in front of him.

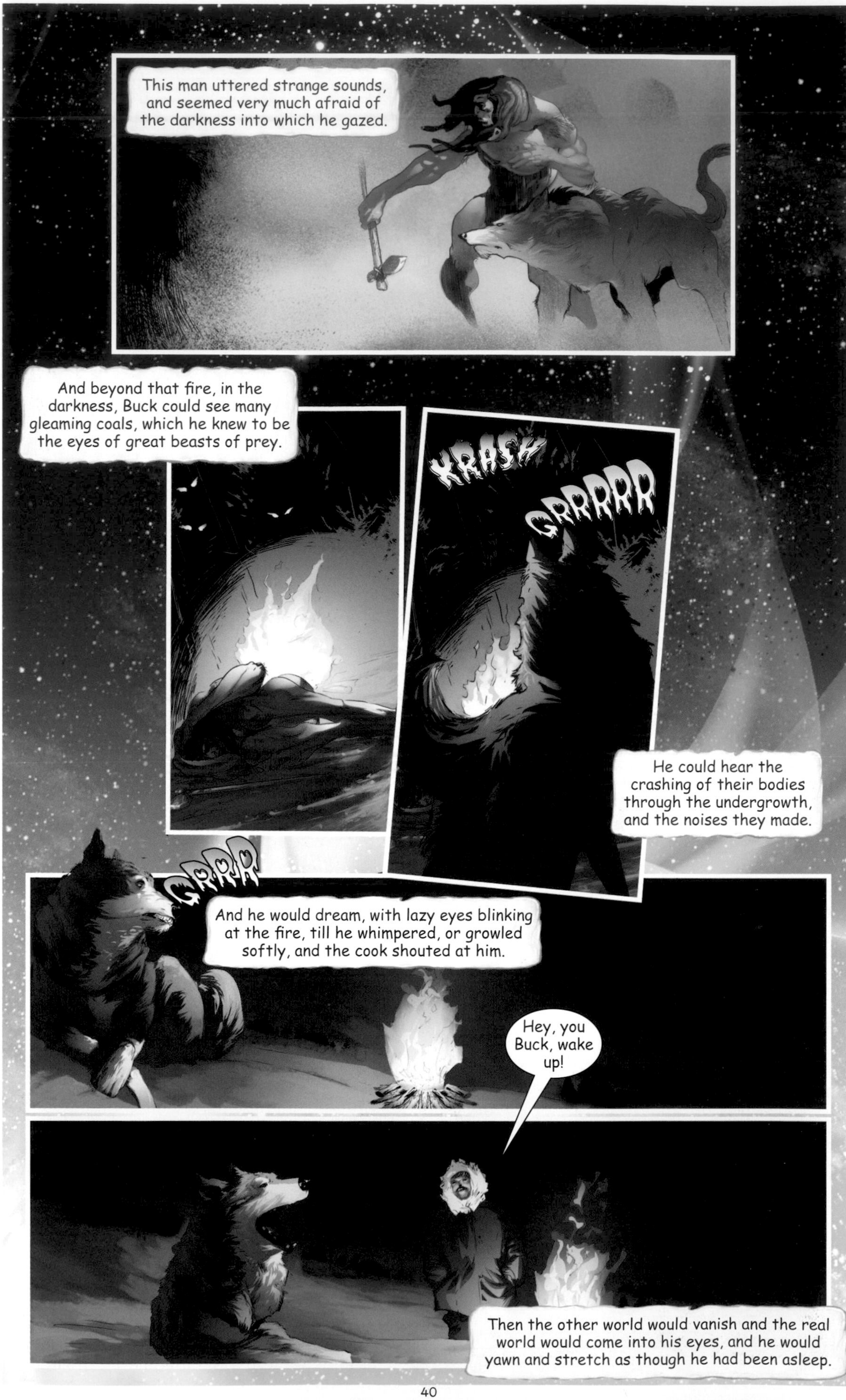
This man uttered strange sounds, and seemed very much afraid of the darkness into which he gazed.
And beyond that fire, in the darkness, Buck could see many gleaming coals, which he knew to be the eyes of great beasts of prey.
KRASH
GRRRRR
He could hear the crashing of their bodies through the undergrowth, and the noises they made.
GRRR
And he would dream, with lazy eyes blinking at the fire, till he whimpered, or growled softly, and the cook shouted at him.
Hey, you Buck, wake up!
Then the other world would vanish and the real world would come into his eyes, and he would yawn and stretch as though he had been asleep.

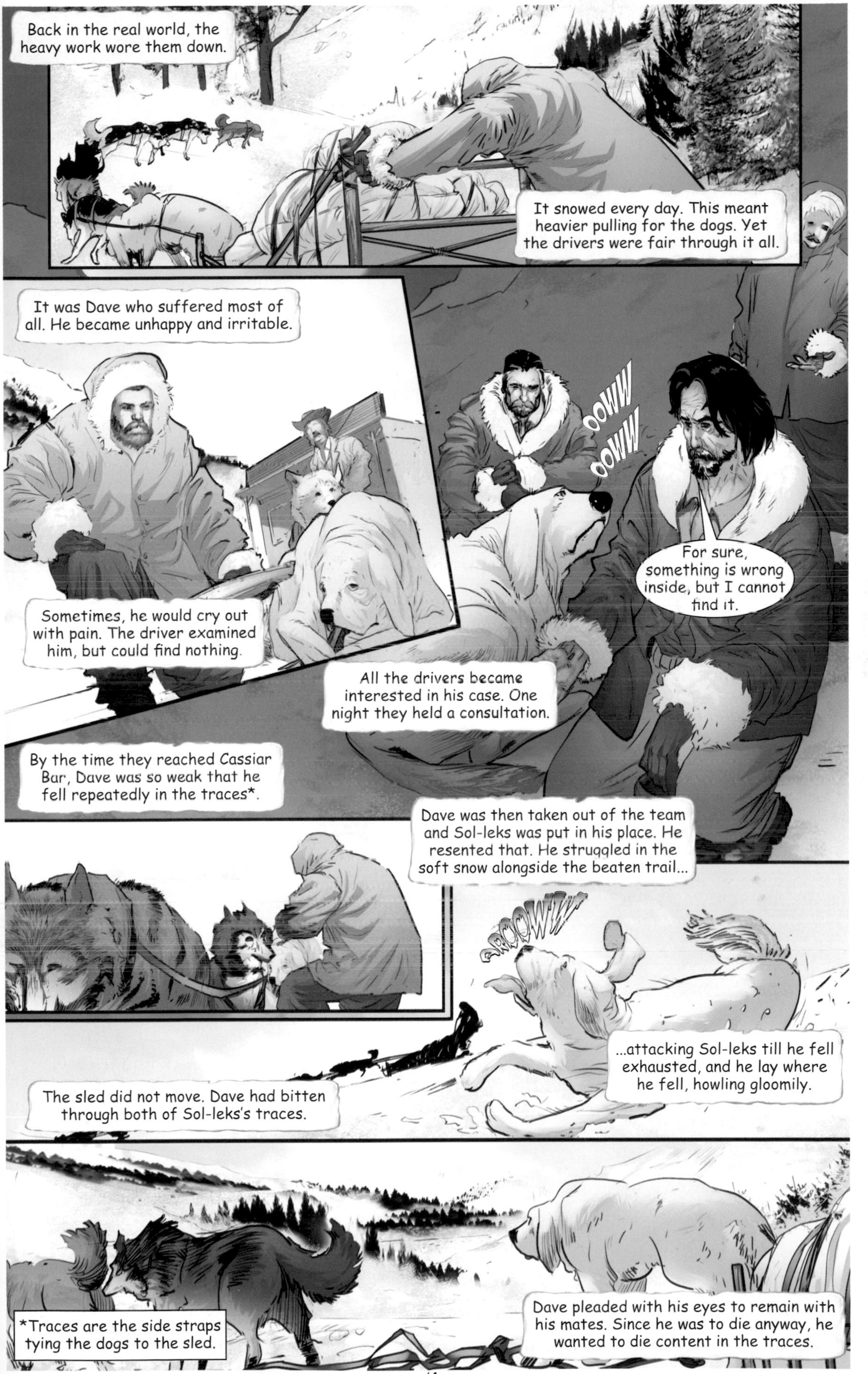
Back in the real world, the heavy work wore them down.
It snowed every day. This meant heavier pulling for the dogs. Yet the drivers were fair through it all.
It was Dave who suffered most of all. He became unhappy and irritable.
OOWW
OOWW
For sure, something is wrong inside, but I cannot find it.
Sometimes, he would cry out with pain. The driver examined him, but could find nothing.
All the drivers became interested in his case. One night they held a consultation.
By the time they reached Cassiar Bar, Dave was so weak that he fell repeatedly in the traces*.
Dave was then taken out of the team and Sol-leks was put in his place. He resented that. He struggled in the soft snow alongside the beaten trail...
...attacking Sol-leks till he fell exhausted, and he lay where he fell, howling gloomily.
The sled did not move. Dave had bitten through both of Sol-leks's traces.
*Traces are the side straps tying the dogs to the sled.
Dave pleaded with his eyes to remain with his mates. Since he was to die anyway, he wanted to die content in the traces.

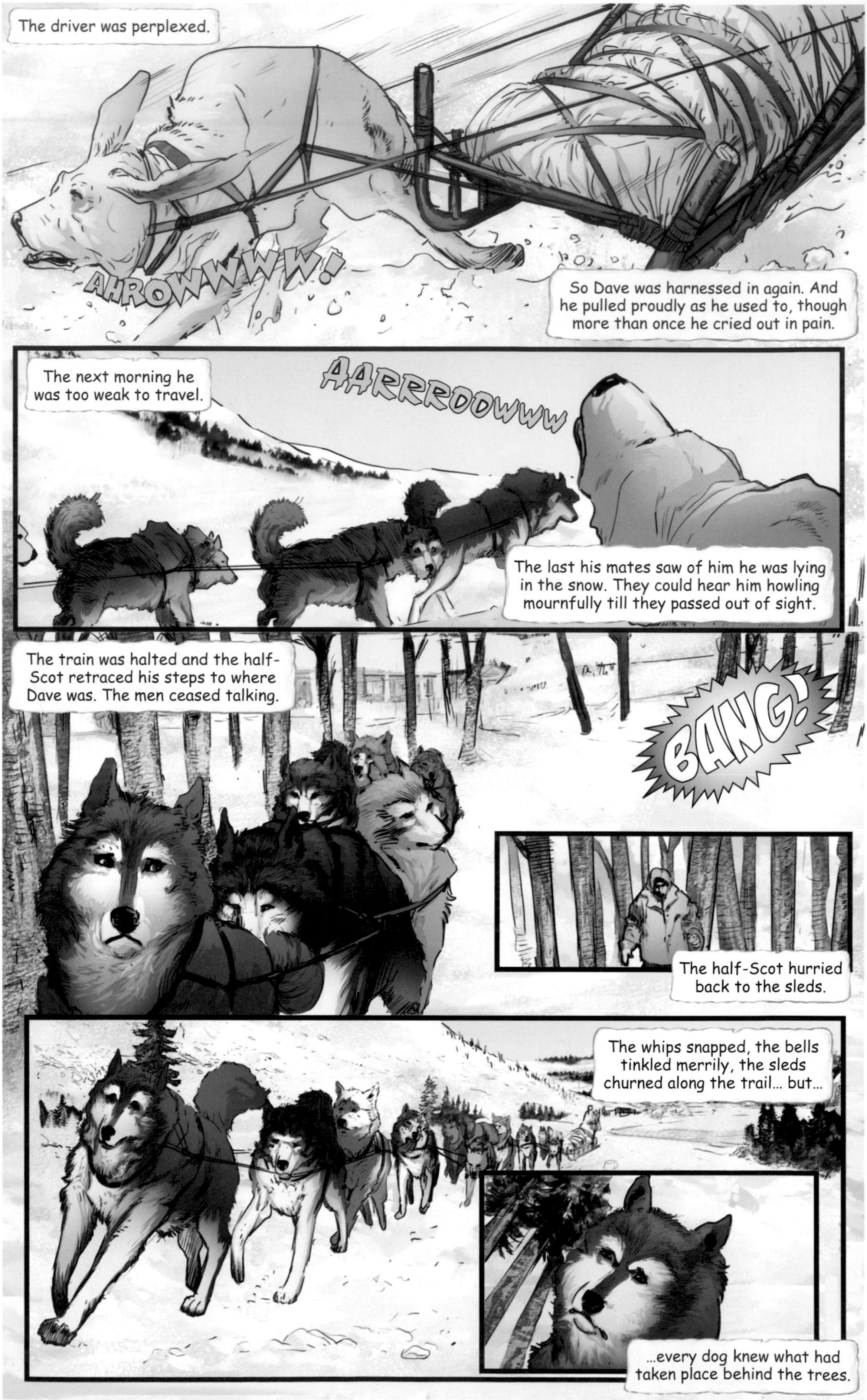

The driver was perplexed.
AHROWWWWW!
So Dave was harnessed in again. And he pulled proudly as he used to, though more than once he cried out in pain.
The next morning he was too weak to travel.
AARRROOWWW
The last his mates saw of him he was lying in the snow. They could hear him howling mournfully till they passed out of sight.
The train was halted and the half-Scot retraced his steps to where Dave was. The men ceased talking.
BANG!
The half-Scot hurried back to the sleds.
The whips snapped, the bells tinkled merrily, the sleds churned along the trail... but...
...every dog knew what had taken place behind the trees.

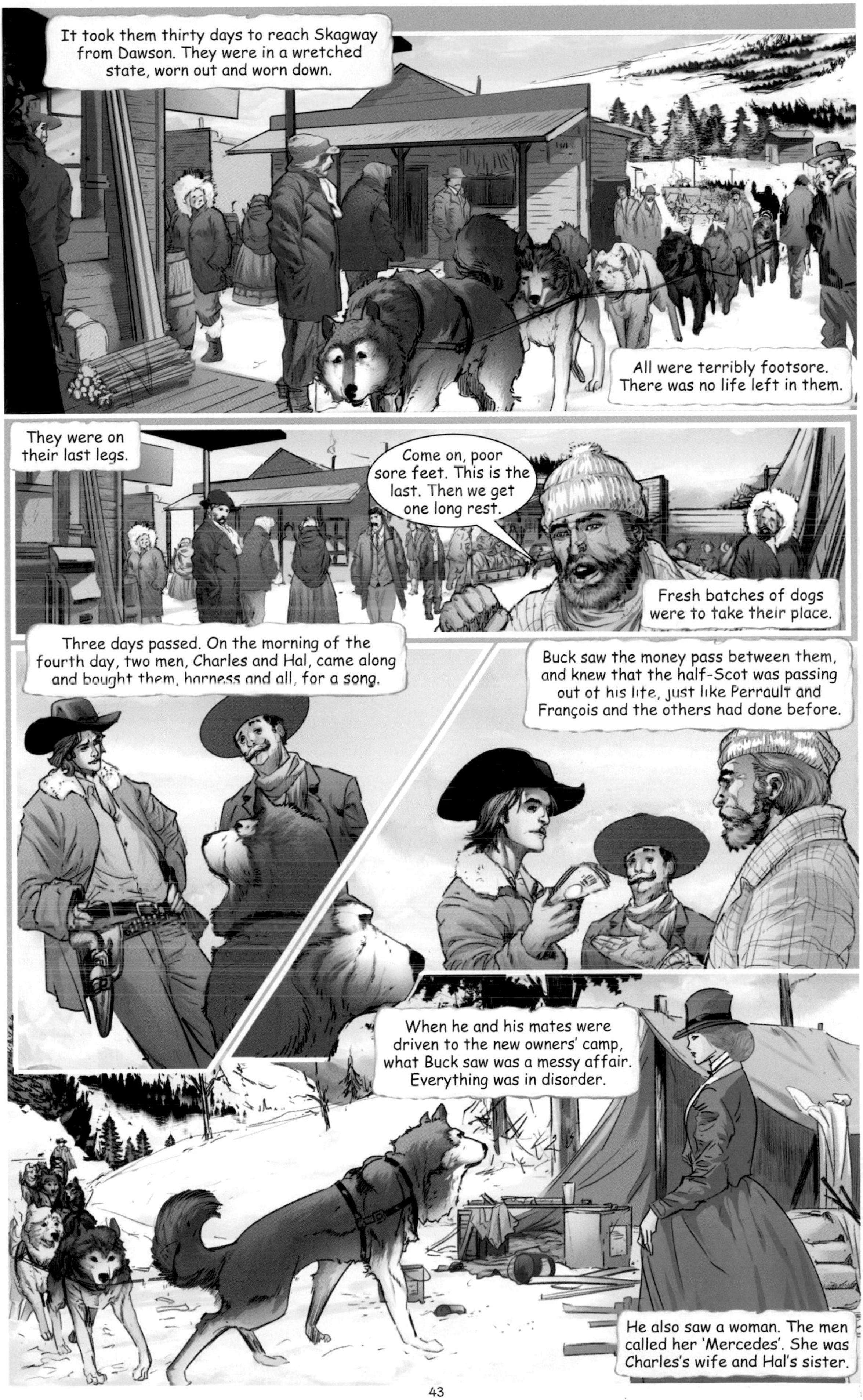
It took them thirty days to reach Skagway from Dawson. They were in a wretched state, worn out and worn down.
All were terribly footsore. There was no life left in them.
They were on their last legs.
Come on, poor sore feet. This is the last. Then we get one long rest.
Fresh batches of dogs were to take their place.
Three days passed. On the morning of the fourth day, two men, Charles and Hal, came along and bought them, harness and all, for a song.
Buck saw the money pass between them, and knew that the half-Scot was passing out of his life, just like Perrault and François and the others had done before.
When he and his mates were driven to the new owners' camp, what Buck saw was a messy affair. Everything was in disorder.
He also saw a woman. The men called her 'Mercedes'. She was Charles's wife and Hal's sister.

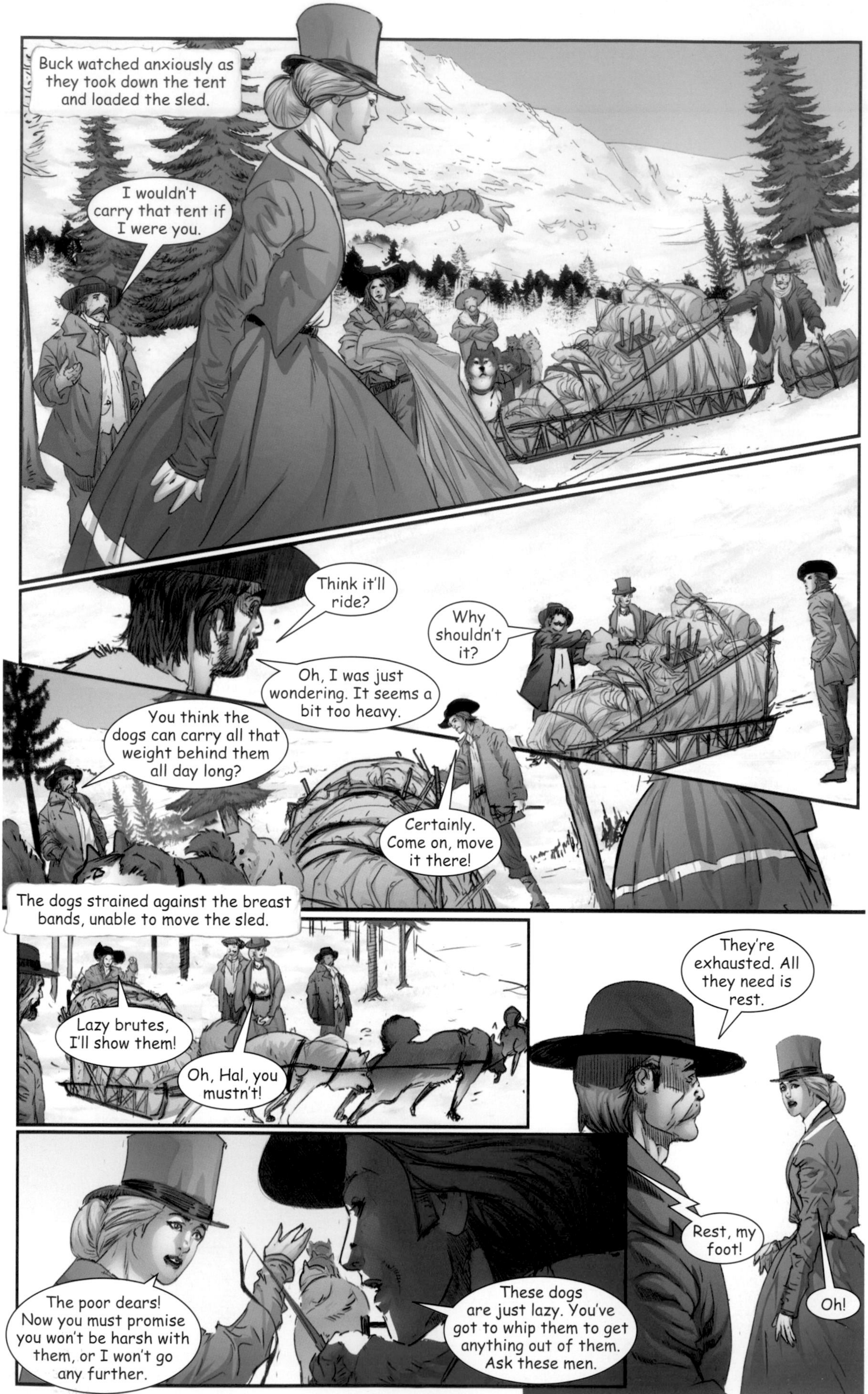

Buck watched anxiously as they took down the tent and loaded the sled.
I wouldn't carry that tent if I were you.
Think it'll ride?
Why shouldn't it?
Oh, I was just wondering. It seems a bit too heavy.
You think the dogs can carry all that weight behind them all day long?
Certainly. Come on, move it there!
The dogs strained against the breast bands, unable to move the sled.
Lazy brutes, I'll show them!
Oh, Hal, you mustn't!
They're exhausted. All they need is rest.
Rest, my foot!
Oh!
The poor dears! Now you must promise you won't be harsh with them, or I won't go any further.
These dogs are just lazy. You've got to whip them to get anything out of them. Ask these men.

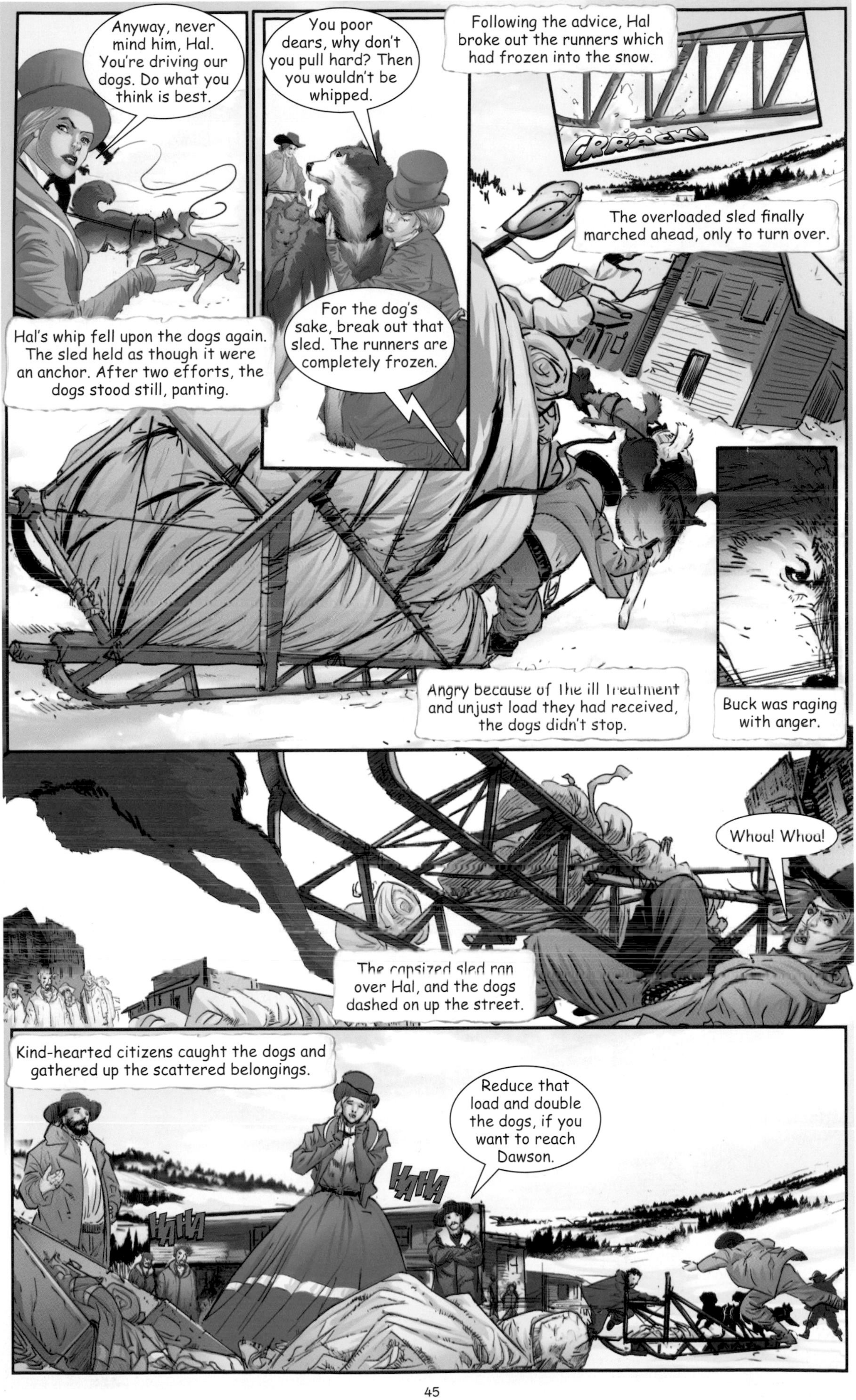
Anyway, never mind him, Hal. You're driving our dogs. Do what you think is best.
You poor dears, why don't you pull hard? Then you wouldn't be whipped.
Hal's whip fell upon the dogs again. The sled held as though it were an anchor. After two efforts, the dogs stood still, panting.
For the dog's sake, break out that sled. The runners are completely frozen.
Following the advice, Hal broke out the runners which had frozen into the snow.
CRRACK!
The overloaded sled finally marched ahead, only to turn over.
Angry because of the ill treatment and unjust load they had received, the dogs didn't stop.
Buck was raging with anger.
Whoa! Whoa!
The capsized sled ran over Hal, and the dogs dashed on up the street.
Kind-hearted citizens caught the dogs and gathered up the scattered belongings.
Reduce that load and double the dogs, if you want to reach Dawson.
HAHA
HAHA

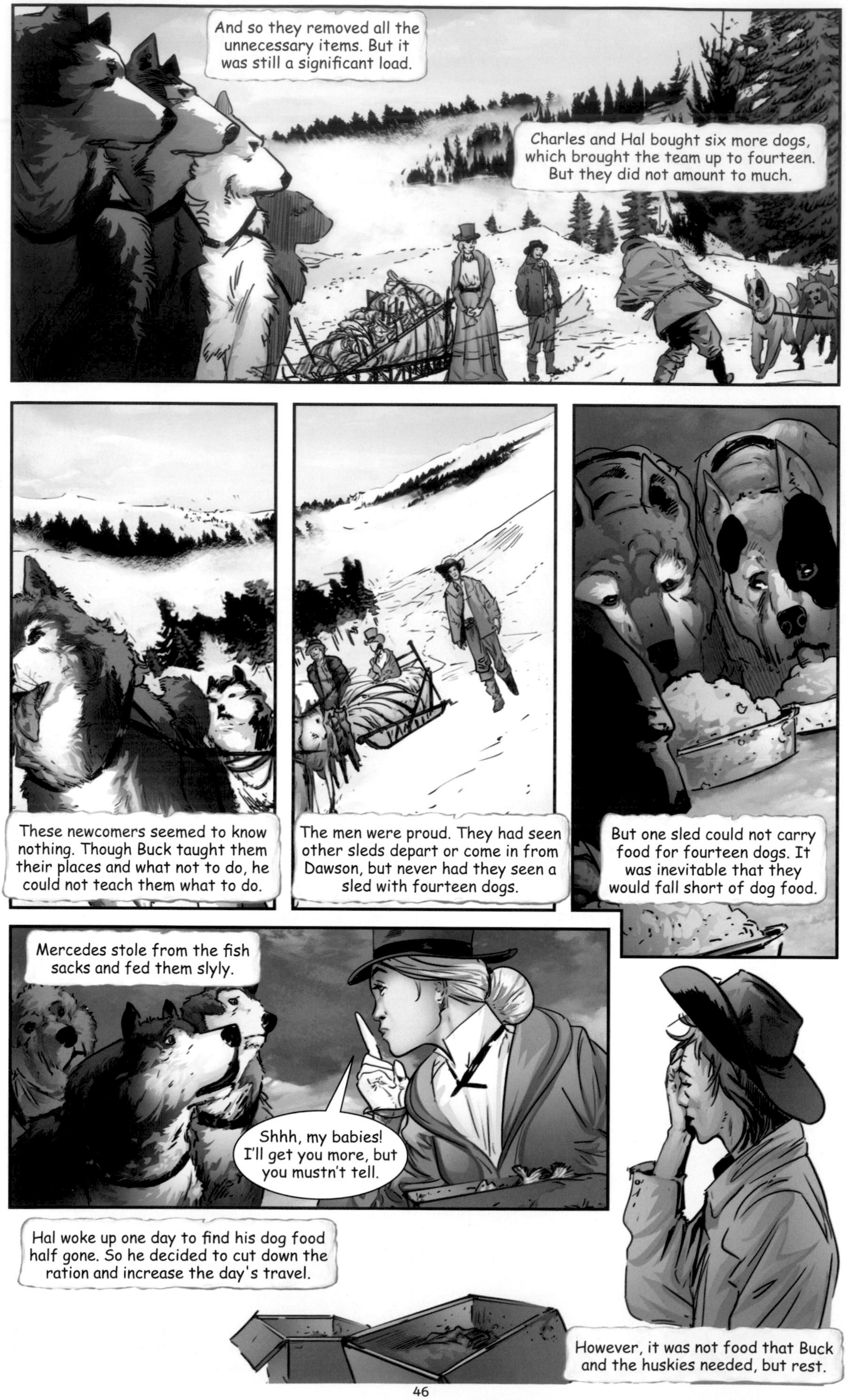

And so they removed all the unnecessary items. But it was still a significant load.
Charles and Hal bought six more dogs, which brought the team up to fourteen. But they did not amount to much.
These newcomers seemed to know nothing. Though Buck taught them their places and what not to do, he could not teach them what to do.
The men were proud. They had seen other sleds depart or come in from Dawson, but never had they seen a sled with fourteen dogs.
But one sled could not carry food for fourteen dogs. It was inevitable that they would fall short of dog food.
Mercedes stole from the fish sacks and fed them slyly.
Shhh, my babies! I'll get you more, but you mustn't tell.
Hal woke up one day to find his dog food half gone. So he decided to cut down the ration and increase the day's travel.
However, it was not food that Buck and the huskies needed, but rest.

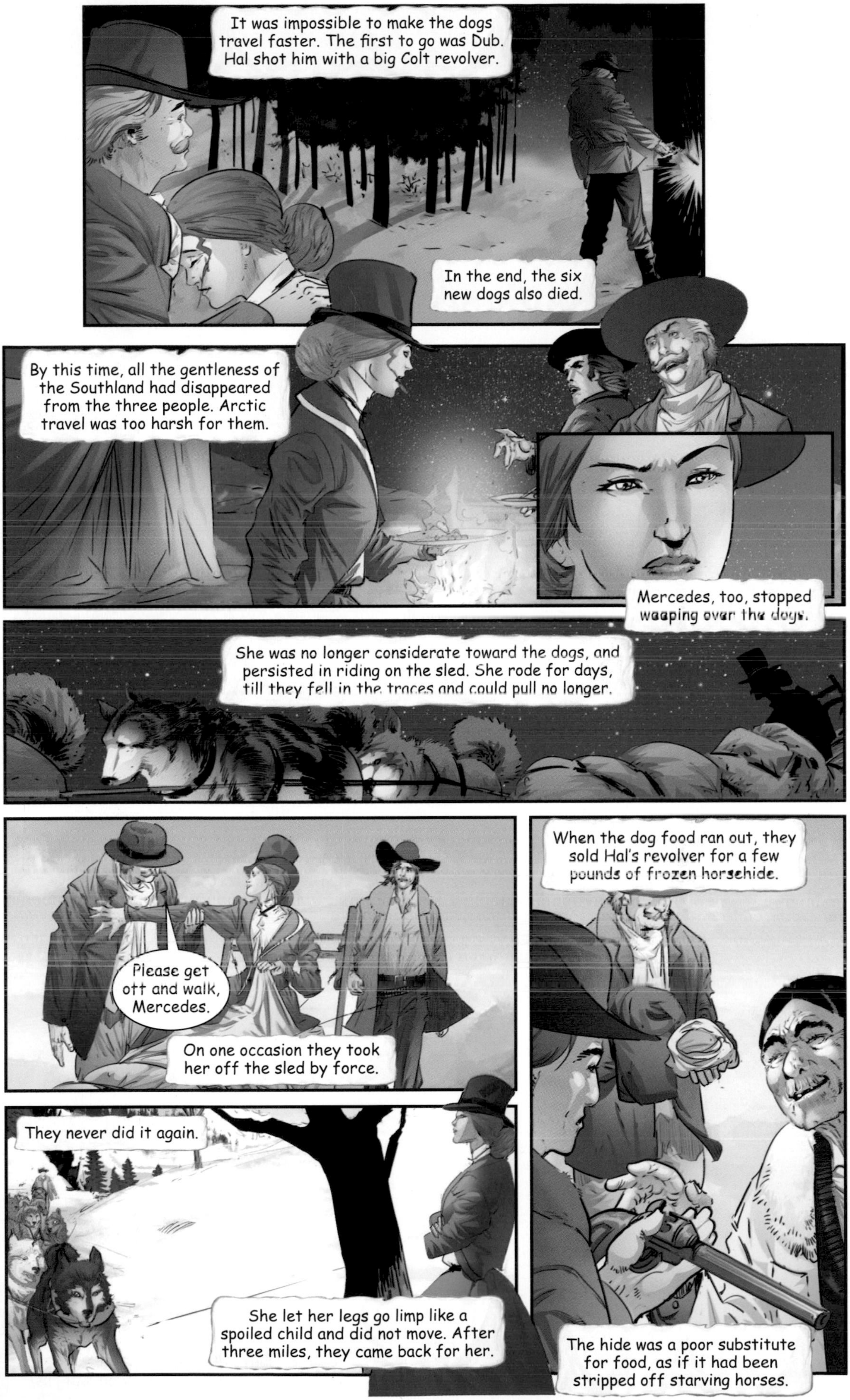
It was impossible to make the dogs travel faster. The first to go was Dub. Hal shot him with a big Colt revolver.
In the end, the six new dogs also died.
By this time, all the gentleness of the Southland had disappeared from the three people. Arctic travel was too harsh for them.
Mercedes, too, stopped weeping over the dogs.
She was no longer considerate toward the dogs, and persisted in riding on the sled. She rode for days, till they fell in the traces and could pull no longer.
Please get off and walk, Mercedes.
On one occasion they took her off the sled by force.
They never did it again.
She let her legs go limp like a spoiled child and did not move. After three miles, they came back for her.
When the dog food ran out, they sold Hal's revolver for a few pounds of frozen horsehide.
The hide was a poor substitute for food, as if it had been stripped off starving horses.

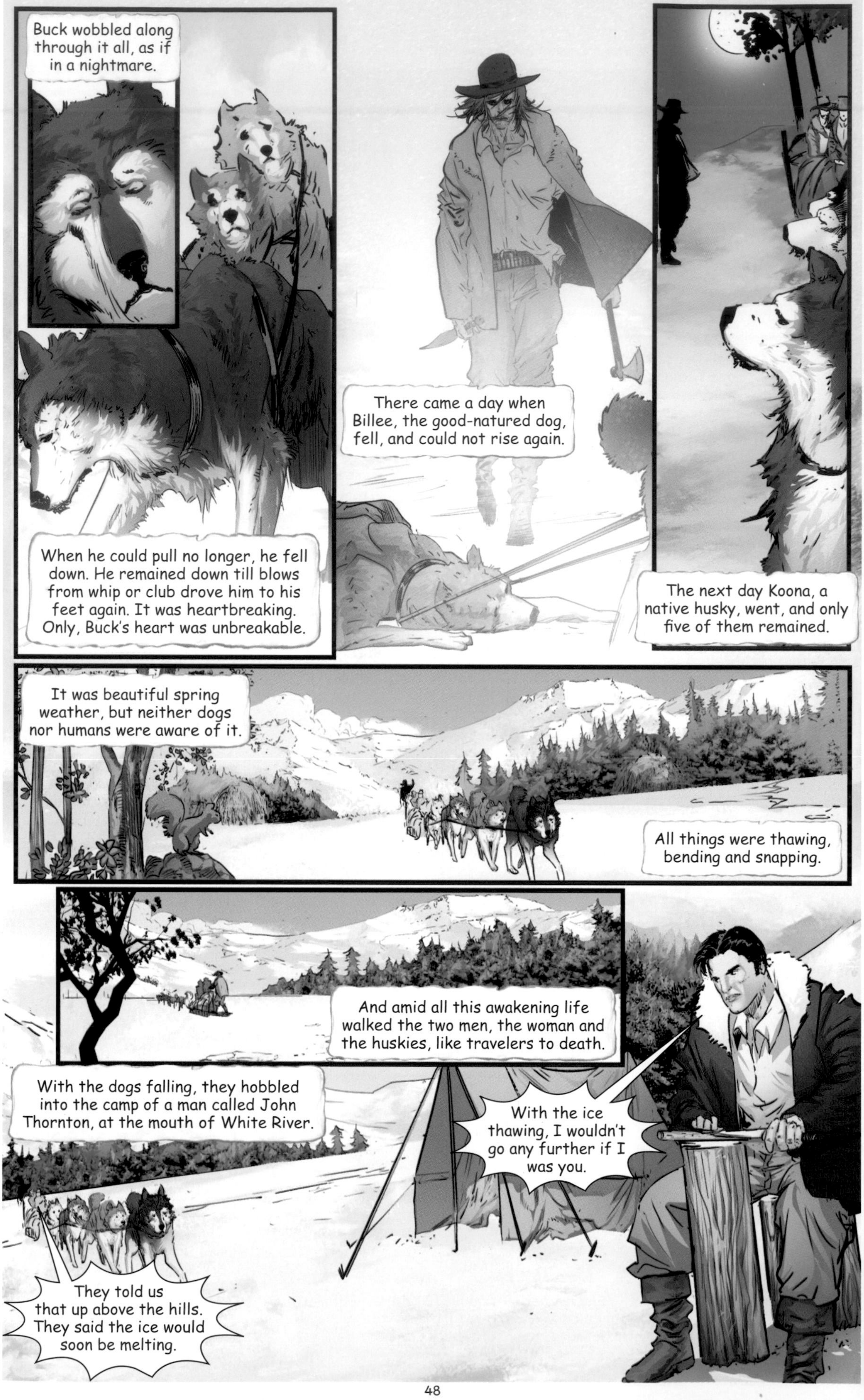

Buck wobbled along through it all, as if in a nightmare.
When he could pull no longer, he fell down. He remained down till blows from whip or club drove him to his feet again. It was heartbreaking. Only, Buck's heart was unbreakable.
There came a day when Billee, the good-natured dog, fell, and could not rise again.
The next day Koona, a native husky, went, and only five of them remained.
It was beautiful spring weather, but neither dogs nor humans were aware of it.
All things were thawing, bending and snapping.
And amid all this awakening life walked the two men, the woman and the huskies, like travelers to death.
With the dogs falling, they hobbled into the camp of a man called John Thornton, at the mouth of White River.
With the ice thawing, I wouldn't go any further if I was you.
They told us that up above the hills. They said the ice would soon be melting.

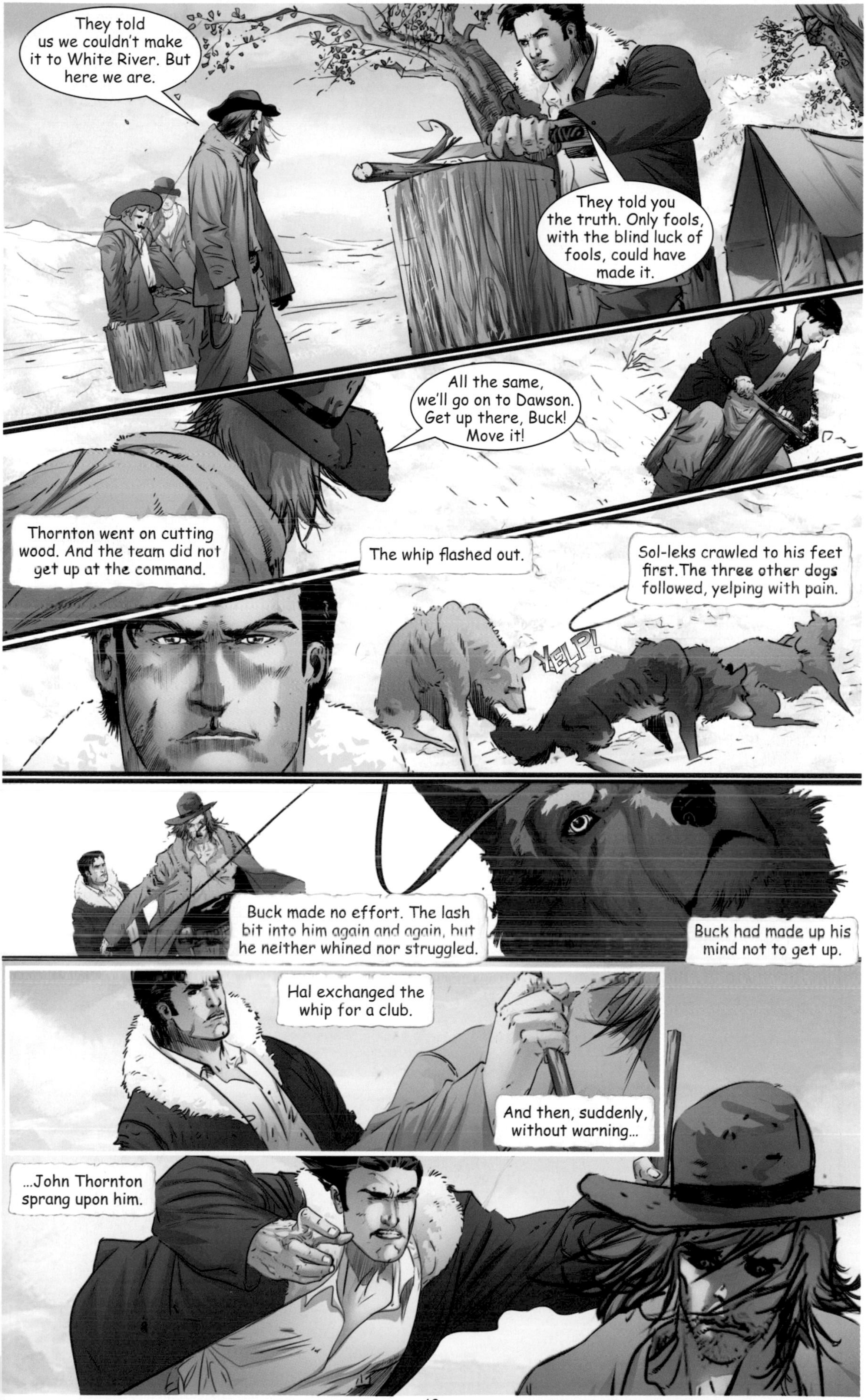
They told us we couldn't make it to White River. But here we are.
They told you the truth. Only fools, with the blind luck of fools, could have made it.
All the same, we'll go on to Dawson. Get up there, Buck! Move it!
Thornton went on cutting wood. And the team did not get up at the command.
The whip flashed out.
Sol-leks crawled to his feet first. The three other dogs followed, yelping with pain.
YELP!
Buck made no effort. The lash bit into him again and again, but he neither whined nor struggled.
Buck had made up his mind not to get up.
Hal exchanged the whip for a club.
And then, suddenly, without warning...
...John Thornton sprang upon him.

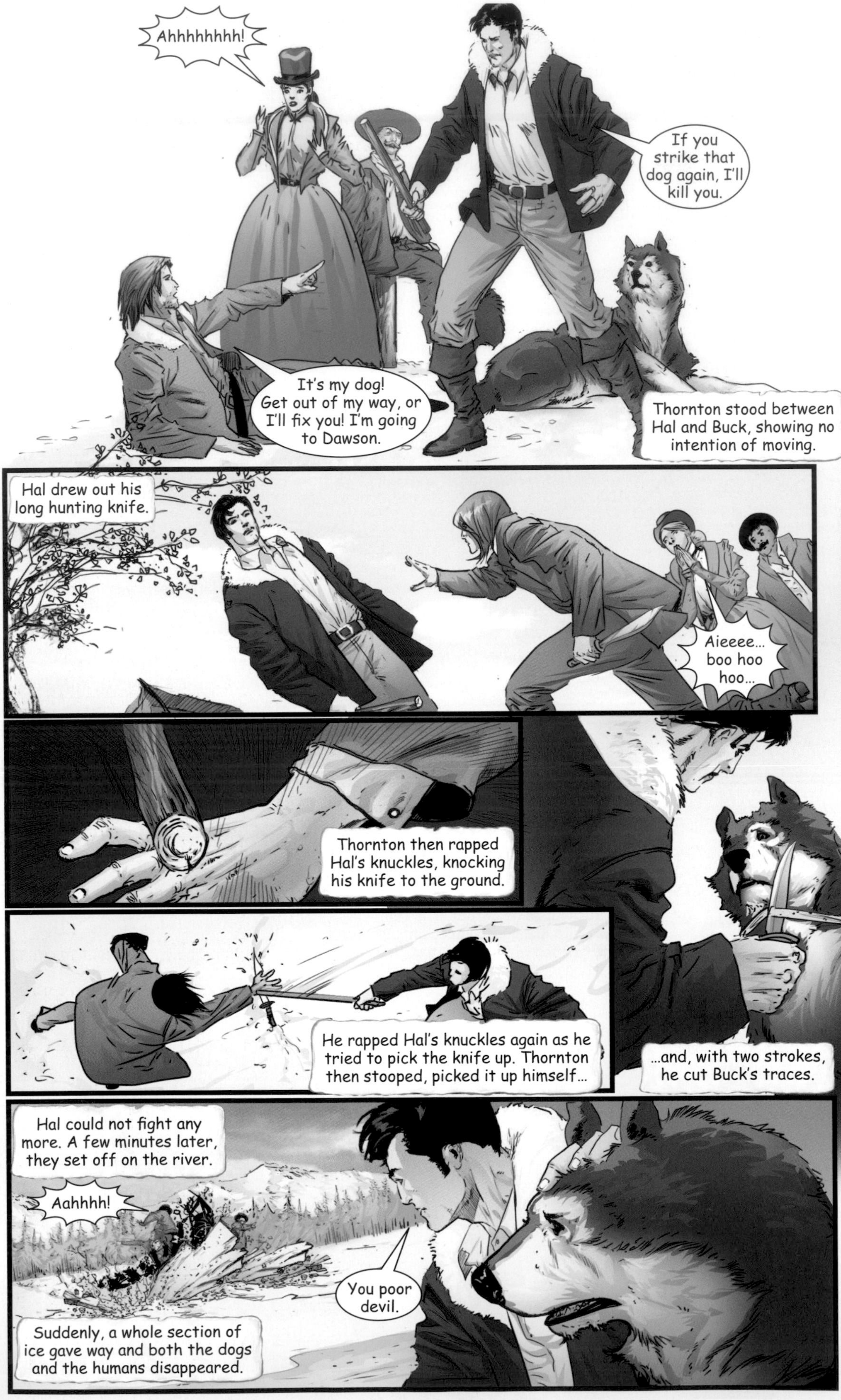
Ahhhhhhhh!
If you strike that dog again, I'll kill you.
It's my dog! Get out of my way, or I'll fix you! I'm going to Dawson.
Thornton stood between Hal and Buck, showing no intention of moving.
Hal drew out his long hunting knife.
Aieeee... boo hoo hoo...
Thornton then rapped Hal's knuckles, knocking his knife to the ground.
He rapped Hal's knuckles again as he tried to pick the knife up. Thornton then stooped, picked it up himself...
...and, with two strokes, he cut Buck's traces.
Hal could not fight any more. A few minutes later, they set off on the river.
Aahhhh!
You poor devil.
Suddenly, a whole section of ice gave way and both the dogs and the humans disappeared.

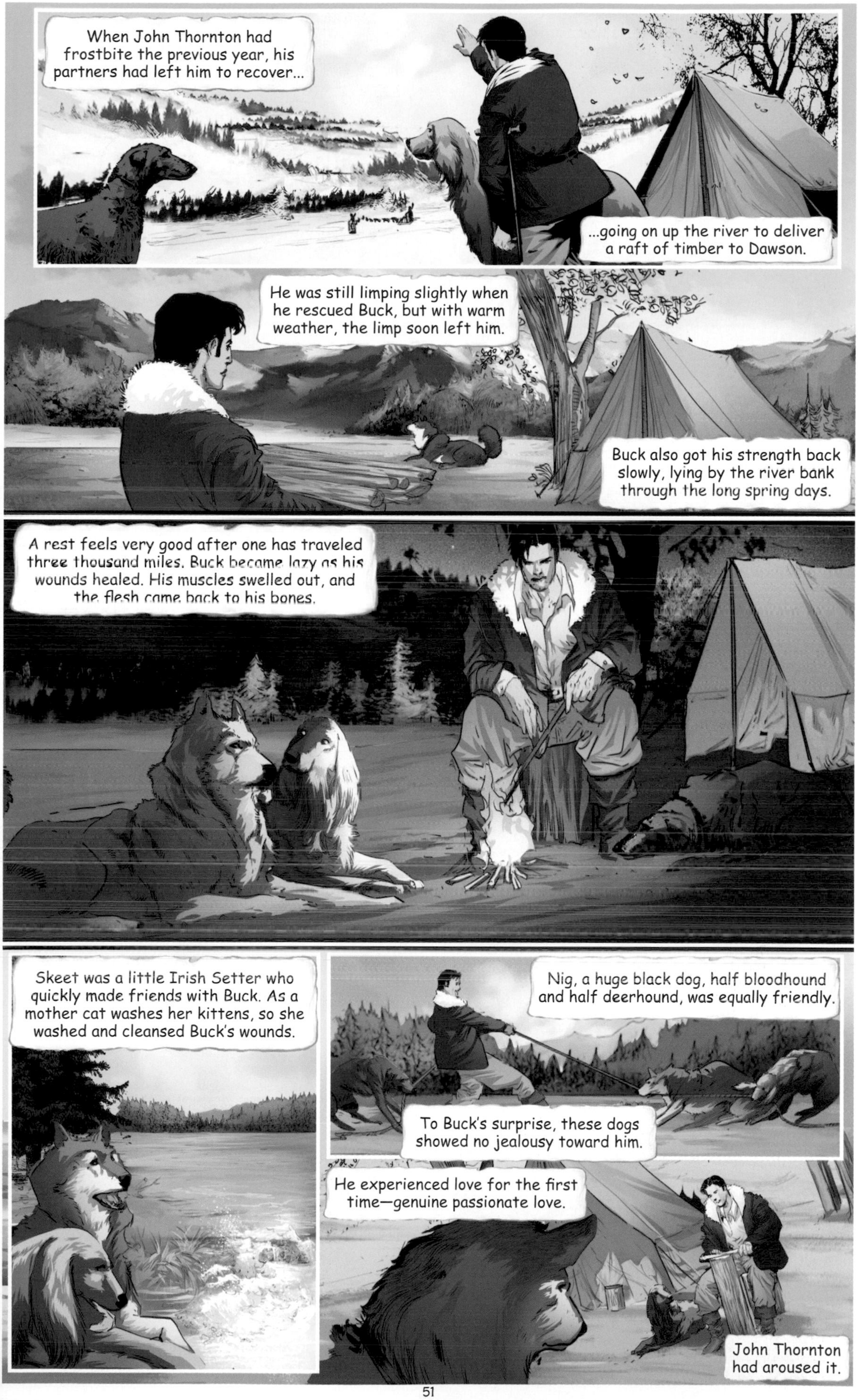
When John Thornton had frostbite the previous year, his partners had left him to recover...
...going on up the river to deliver a raft of timber to Dawson.
He was still limping slightly when he rescued Buck, but with warm weather, the limp soon left him.
Buck also got his strength back slowly, lying by the river bank through the long spring days.
A rest feels very good after one has traveled three thousand miles. Buck became lazy as his wounds healed. His muscles swelled out, and the flesh came back to his bones.
Skeet was a little Irish Setter who quickly made friends with Buck. As a mother cat washes her kittens, so she washed and cleansed Buck's wounds.
Nig, a huge black dog, half bloodhound and half deerhound, was equally friendly.
To Buck's surprise, these dogs showed no jealousy toward him.
He experienced love for the first time—genuine passionate love.
John Thornton had aroused it.

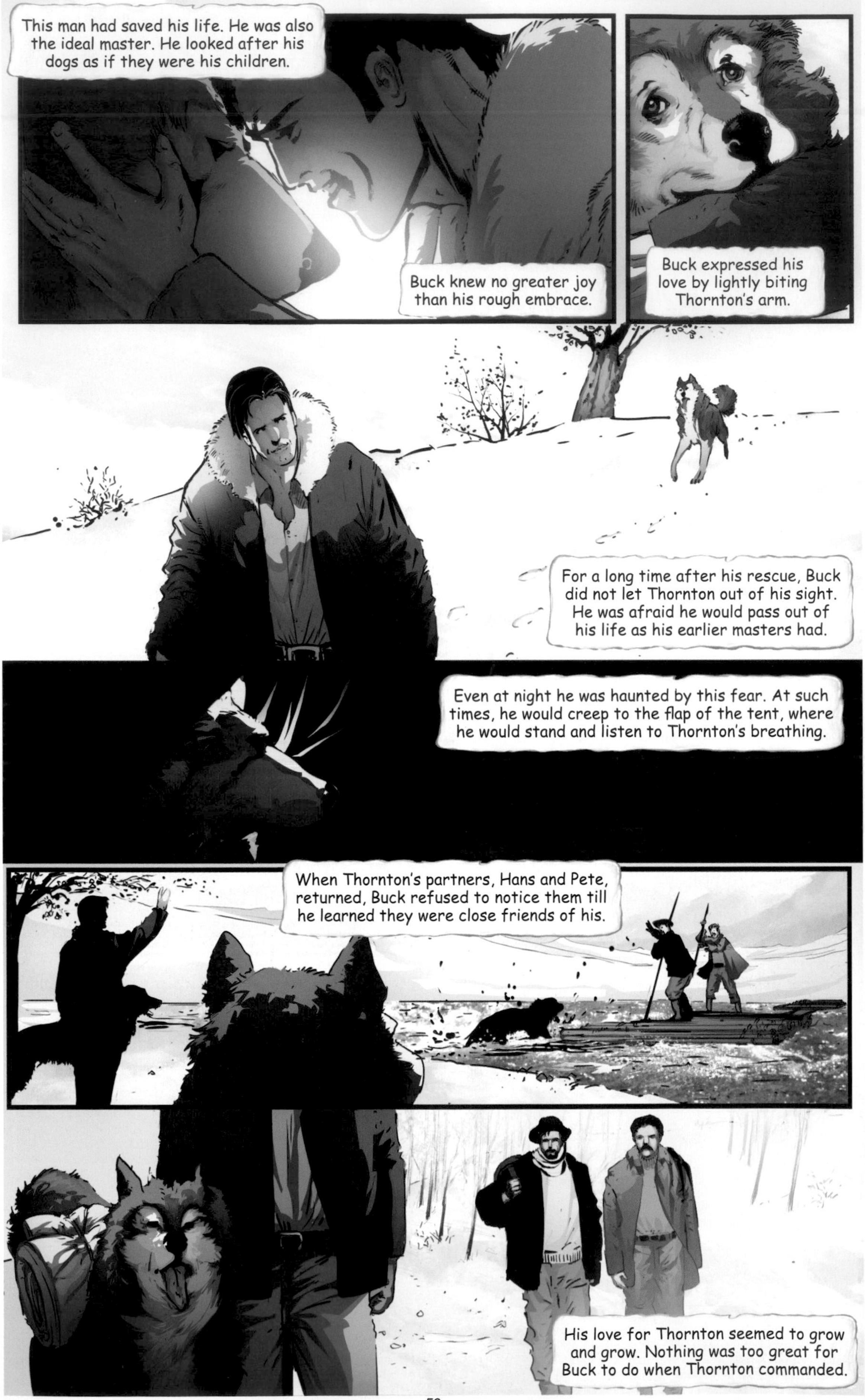
This man had saved his life. He was also the ideal master. He looked after his dogs as if they were his children.
Buck knew no greater joy than his rough embrace.
Buck expressed his love by lightly biting Thornton's arm.
For a long time after his rescue, Buck did not let Thornton out of his sight. He was afraid he would pass out of his life as his earlier masters had.
Even at night he was haunted by this fear. At such times, he would creep to the flap of the tent, where he would stand and listen to Thornton's breathing.
When Thornton's partners, Hans and Pete, returned, Buck refused to notice them till he learned they were close friends of his.
His love for Thornton seemed to grow and grow. Nothing was too great for Buck to do when Thornton commanded.

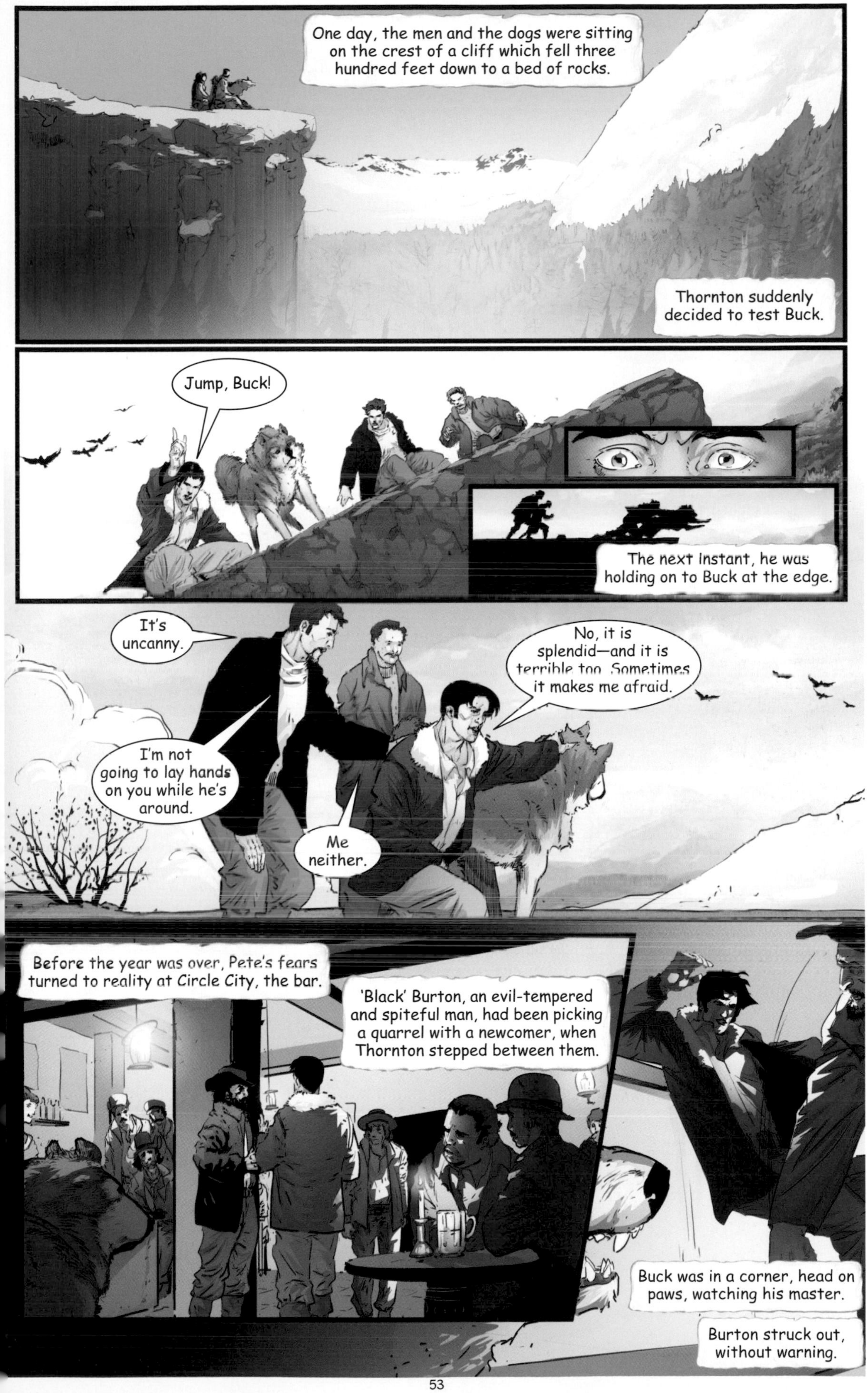
One day, the men and the dogs were sitting on the crest of a cliff which fell three hundred feet down to a bed of rocks.
Thornton suddenly decided to test Buck.
Jump, Buck!
The next instant, he was holding on to Buck at the edge.
It's uncanny.
No, it is splendid—and it is terrible too. Sometimes it makes me afraid.
I'm not going to lay hands on you while he's around.
Me neither.
Before the year was over, Pete's fears turned to reality at Circle City, the bar.
'Black' Burton, an evil-tempered and spiteful man, had been picking a quarrel with a newcomer, when Thornton stepped between them.
Buck was in a corner, head on paws, watching his master.
Burton struck out, without warning.

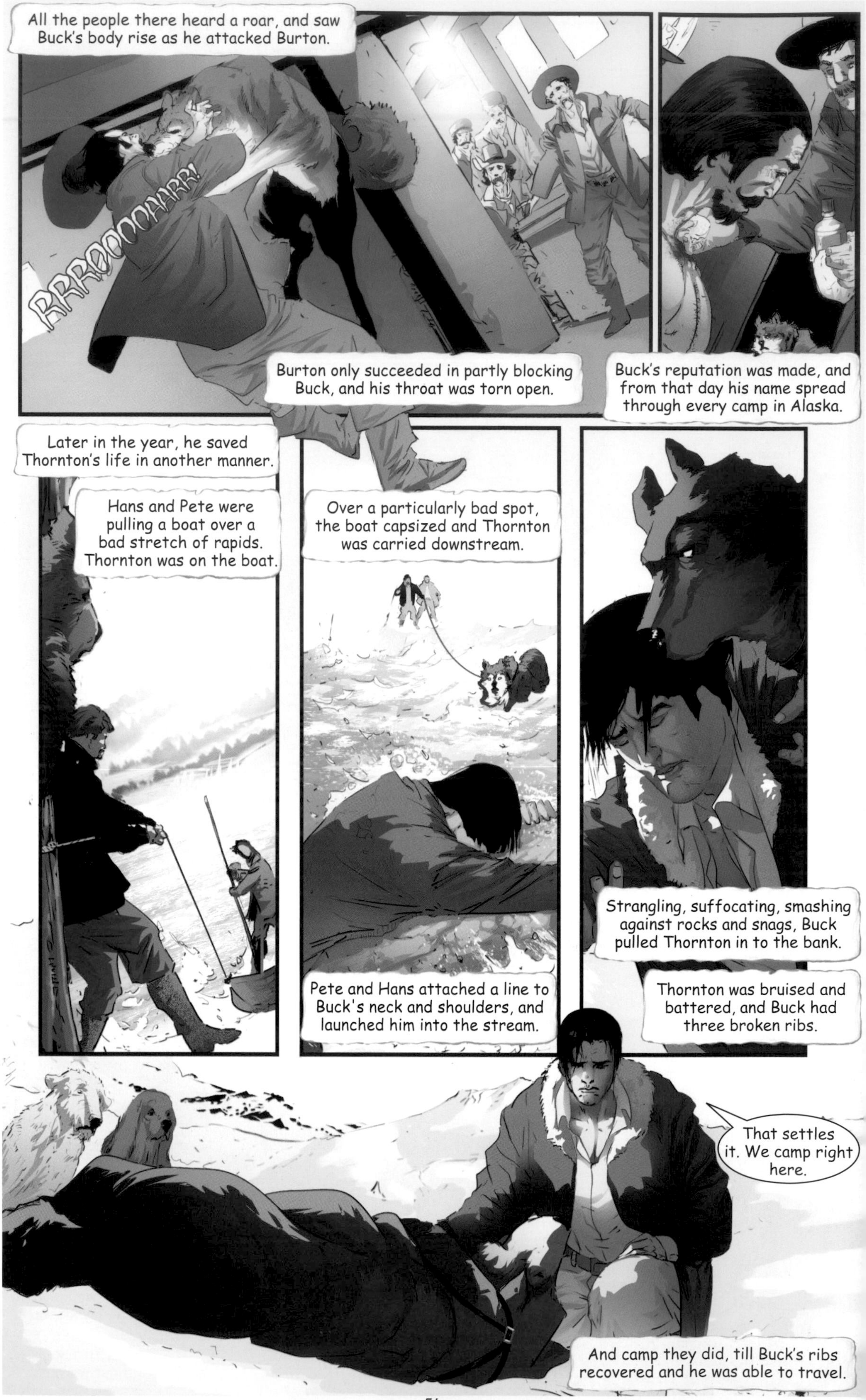
All the people there heard a roar, and saw Buck's body rise as he attacked Burton.
RRROOOOAARR!
Burton only succeeded in partly blocking Buck, and his throat was torn open.
Buck's reputation was made, and from that day his name spread through every camp in Alaska.
Later in the year, he saved Thornton's life in another manner.
Hans and Pete were pulling a boat over a bad stretch of rapids. Thornton was on the boat.
Over a particularly bad spot, the boat capsized and Thornton was carried downstream.
Pete and Hans attached a line to Buck's neck and shoulders, and launched him into the stream.
Strangling, suffocating, smashing against rocks and snags, Buck pulled Thornton in to the bank.
Thornton was bruised and battered, and Buck had three broken ribs.
That settles it. We camp right here.
And camp they did, till Buck's ribs recovered and he was able to travel.

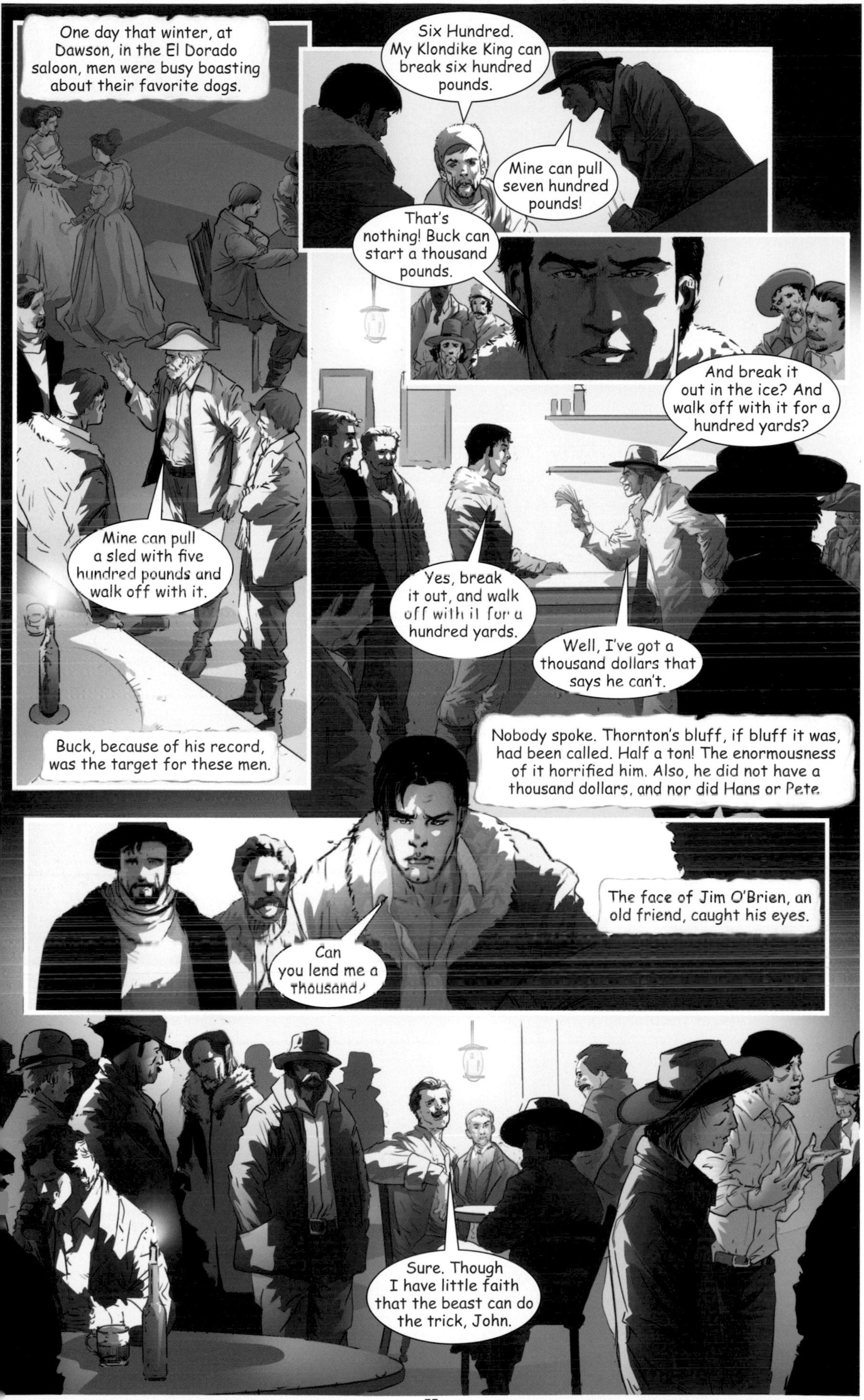
One day that winter, at Dawson, in the El Dorado saloon, men were busy boasting about their favorite dogs.
Buck, because of his record, was the target for these men.
Mine can pull a sled with five hundred pounds and walk off with it.
Six Hundred. My Klondike King can break six hundred pounds.
Mine can pull seven hundred pounds!
That's nothing! Buck can start a thousand pounds.
And break it out in the ice? And walk off with it for a hundred yards?
Yes, break it out, and walk off with it for a hundred yards.
Well, I've got a thousand dollars that says he can't.
Nobody spoke. Thornton's bluff, if bluff it was, had been called. Half a ton! The enormousness of it horrified him. Also, he did not have a thousand dollars, and nor did Hans or Pete.
The face of Jim O'Brien, an old friend, caught his eyes.
Can you lend me a thousand?
Sure. Though I have little faith that the beast can do the trick, John.

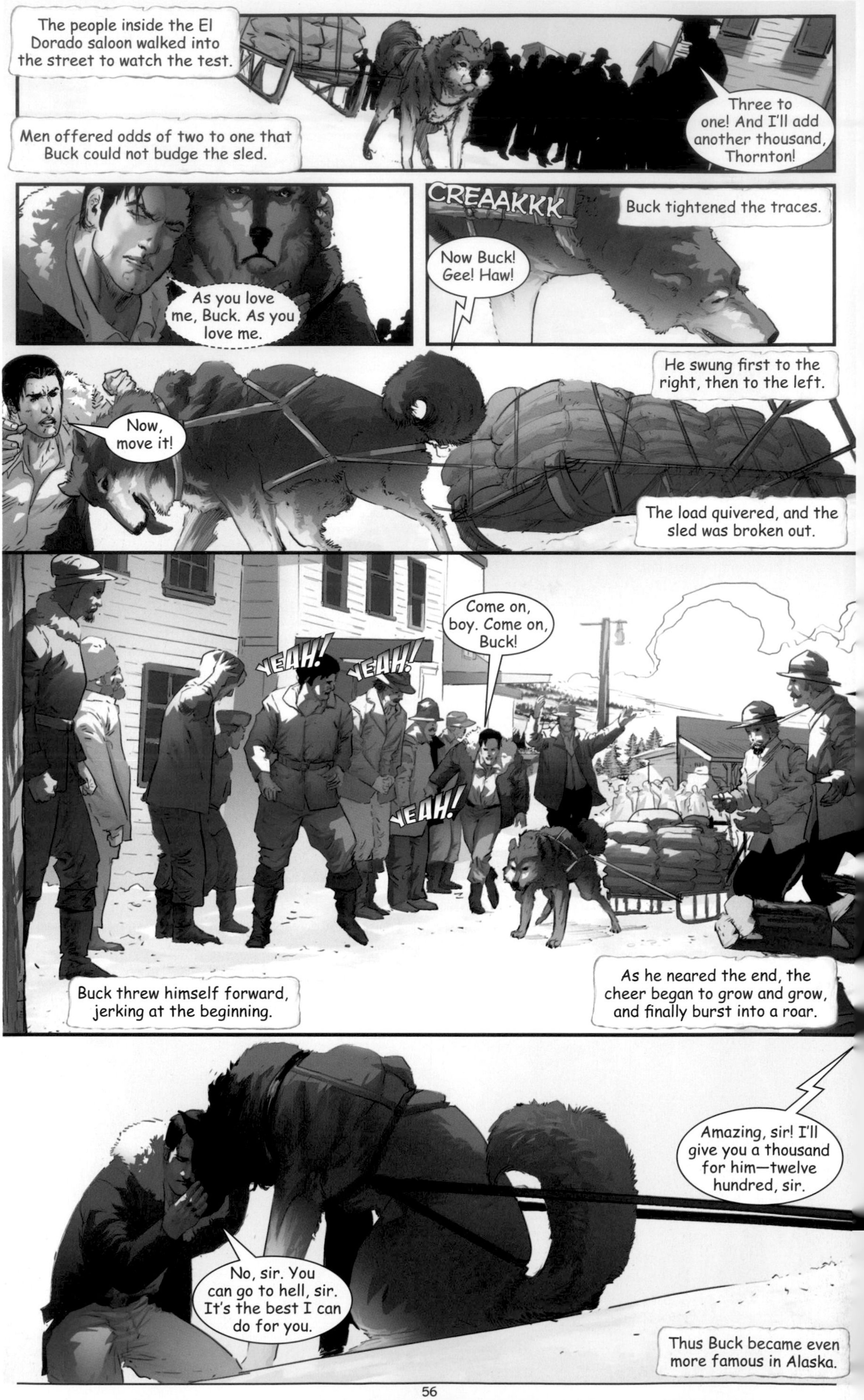

The people inside the El Dorado saloon walked into the street to watch the test.
Men offered odds of two to one that Buck could not budge the sled.
Three to one! And I'll add another thousand, Thornton!
As you love me, Buck. As you love me.
CREAAKKK
Buck tightened the traces.
Now Buck! Gee! Haw!
He swung first to the right, then to the left.
Now, move it!
The load quivered, and the sled was broken out.
YEAH!
YEAH!
Come on, boy. Come on, Buck!
YEAH!
Buck threw himself forward, jerking at the beginning.
As he neared the end, the cheer began to grow and grow, and finally burst into a roar.
Amazing, sir! I'll give you a thousand for him—twelve hundred, sir.
No, sir. You can go to hell, sir. It's the best I can do for you.
Thus Buck became even more famous in Alaska.

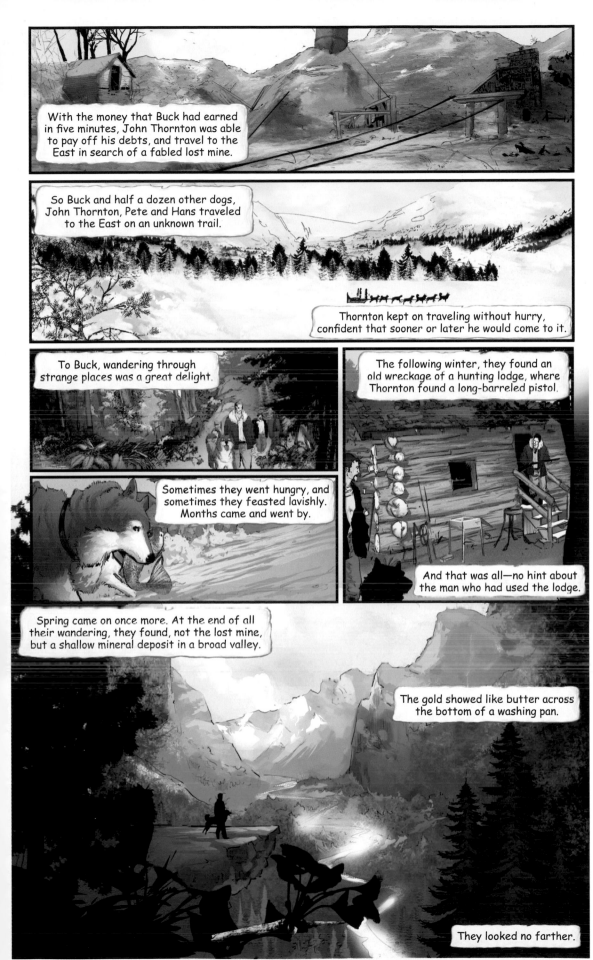

With the money that Buck had earned in five minutes, John Thornton was able to pay off his debts, and travel to the East in search of a fabled lost mine.

So Buck and half a dozen other dogs, John Thornton, Pete and Hans traveled to the East on an unknown trail.

Thornton kept on traveling without hurry, confident that sooner or later he would come to it.

To Buck, wandering through strange places was a great delight.

The following winter, they found an old wreckage of a hunting lodge, where Thornton found a long-barreled pistol.

Sometimes they went hungry, and sometimes they feasted lavishly. Months came and went by.

And that was all—no hint about the man who had used the lodge.

Spring came on once more. At the end of all their wandering, they found, not the lost mine, but a shallow mineral deposit in a broad valley.

The gold showed like butter across the bottom of a washing pan.

They looked no farther.

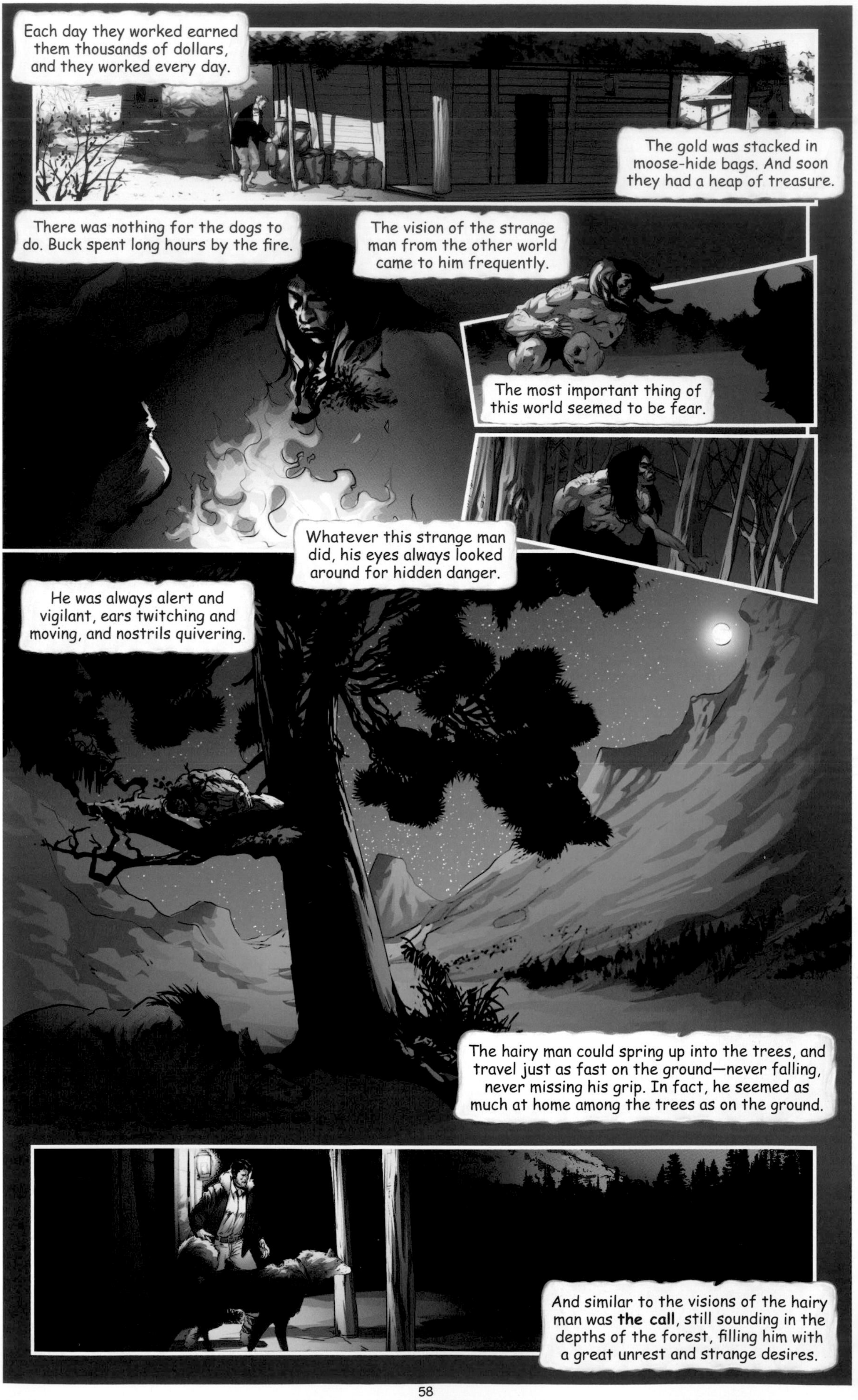
Each day they worked earned them thousands of dollars, and they worked every day.
The gold was stacked in moose-hide bags. And soon they had a heap of treasure.
There was nothing for the dogs to do. Buck spent long hours by the fire.
The vision of the strange man from the other world came to him frequently.
The most important thing of this world seemed to be fear.
Whatever this strange man did, his eyes always looked around for hidden danger.
He was always alert and vigilant, ears twitching and moving, and nostrils quivering.
The hairy man could spring up into the trees, and travel just as fast on the ground—never falling, never missing his grip. In fact, he seemed as much at home among the trees as on the ground.
And similar to the visions of the hairy man was **the call**, still sounding in the depths of the forest, filling him with a great unrest and strange desires.

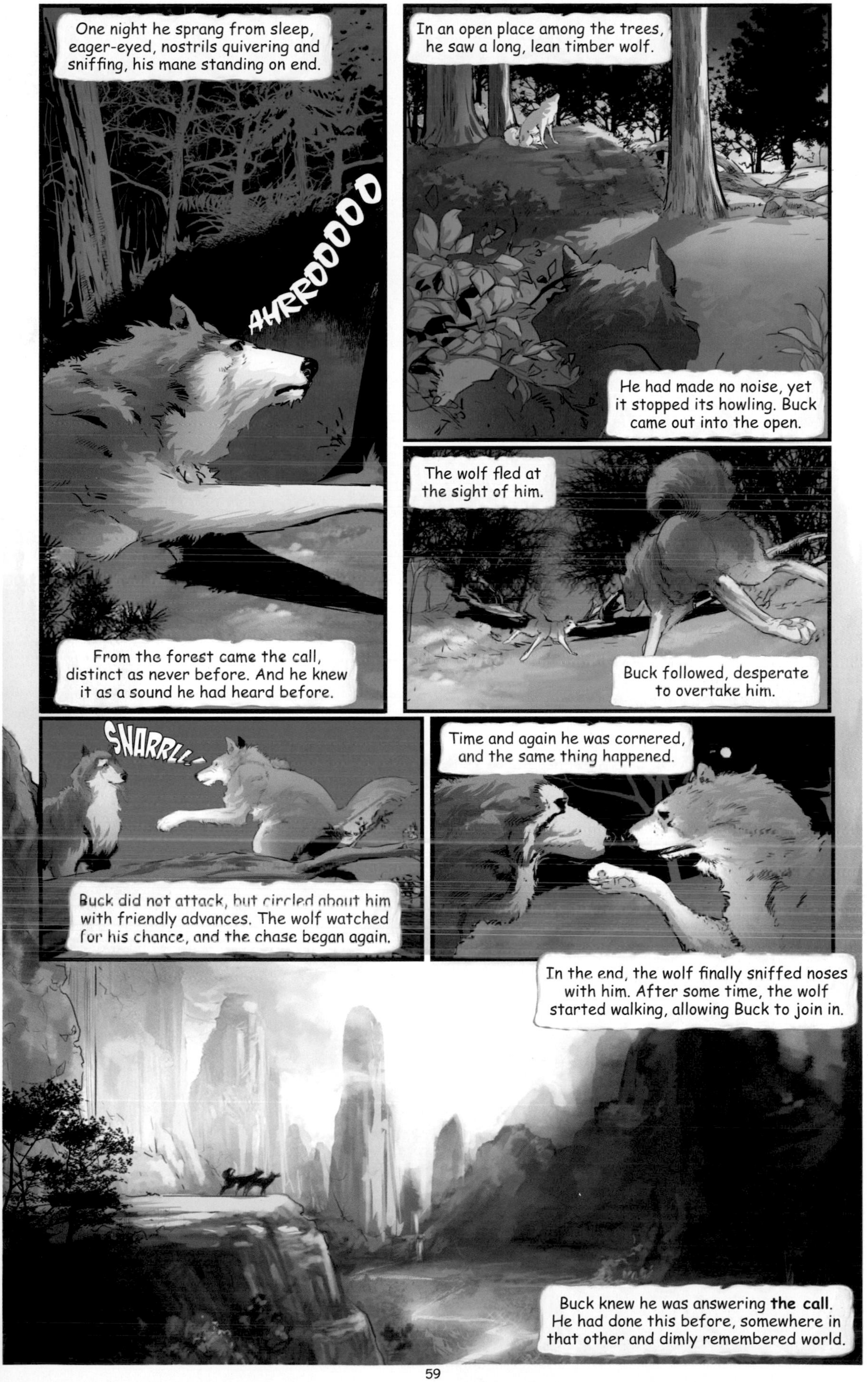
One night he sprang from sleep, eager-eyed, nostrils quivering and sniffing, his mane standing on end.
AHRROOOOO
From the forest came the call, distinct as never before. And he knew it as a sound he had heard before.
In an open place among the trees, he saw a long, lean timber wolf.
He had made no noise, yet it stopped its howling. Buck came out into the open.
The wolf fled at the sight of him.
Buck followed, desperate to overtake him.
SNARRLL!
Buck did not attack, but circled about him with friendly advances. The wolf watched for his chance, and the chase began again.
Time and again he was cornered, and the same thing happened.
In the end, the wolf finally sniffed noses with him. After some time, the wolf started walking, allowing Buck to join in.
Buck knew he was answering **the call**. He had done this before, somewhere in that other and dimly remembered world.

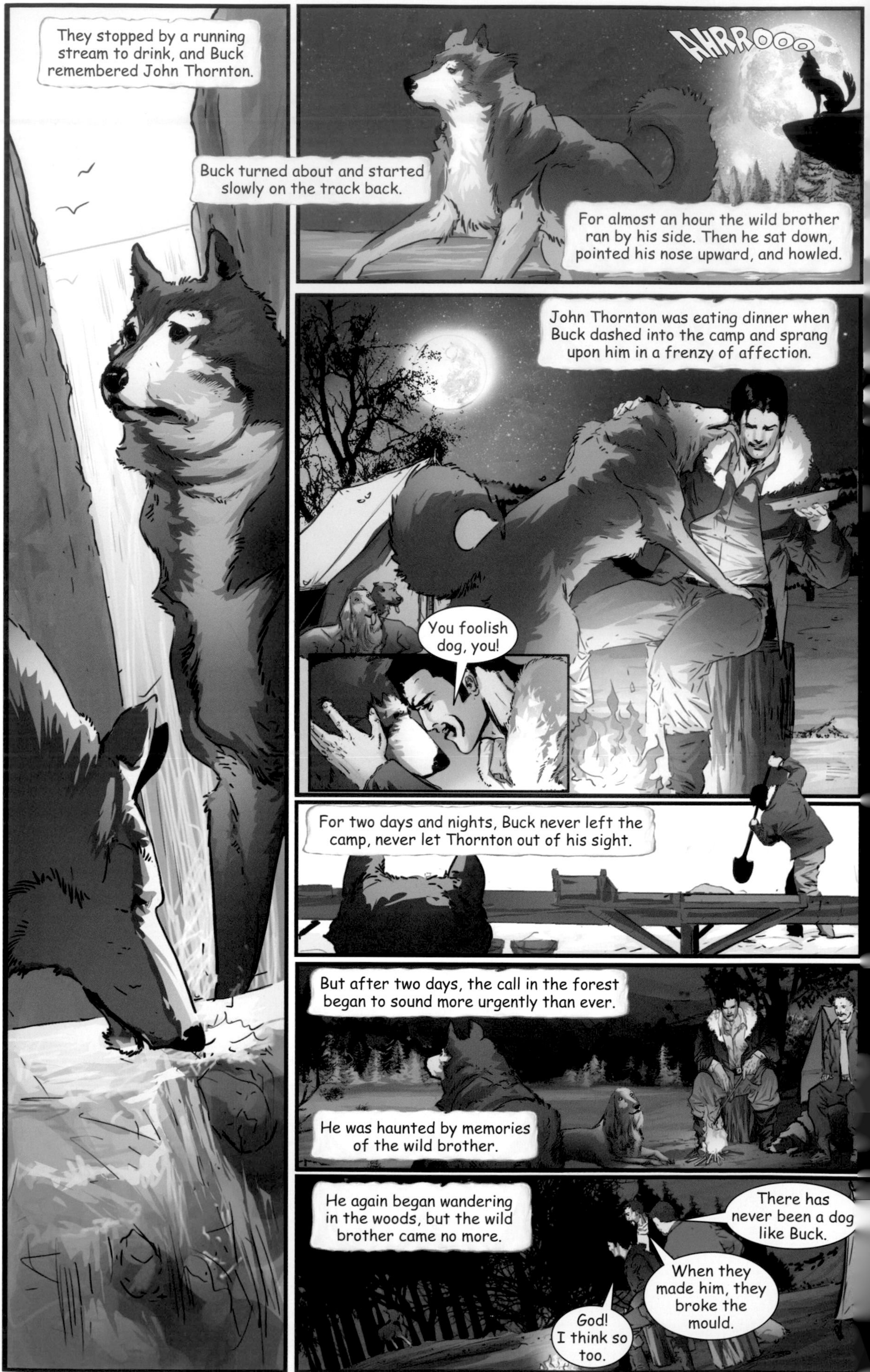
They stopped by a running stream to drink, and Buck remembered John Thornton.
Buck turned about and started slowly on the track back.
AHRROOO
For almost an hour the wild brother ran by his side. Then he sat down, pointed his nose upward, and howled.
John Thornton was eating dinner when Buck dashed into the camp and sprang upon him in a frenzy of affection.
You foolish dog, you!
For two days and nights, Buck never left the camp, never let Thornton out of his sight.
But after two days, the call in the forest began to sound more urgently than ever.
He was haunted by memories of the wild brother.
He again began wandering in the woods, but the wild brother came no more.
There has never been a dog like Buck.
When they made him, they broke the mould.
God! I think so too.

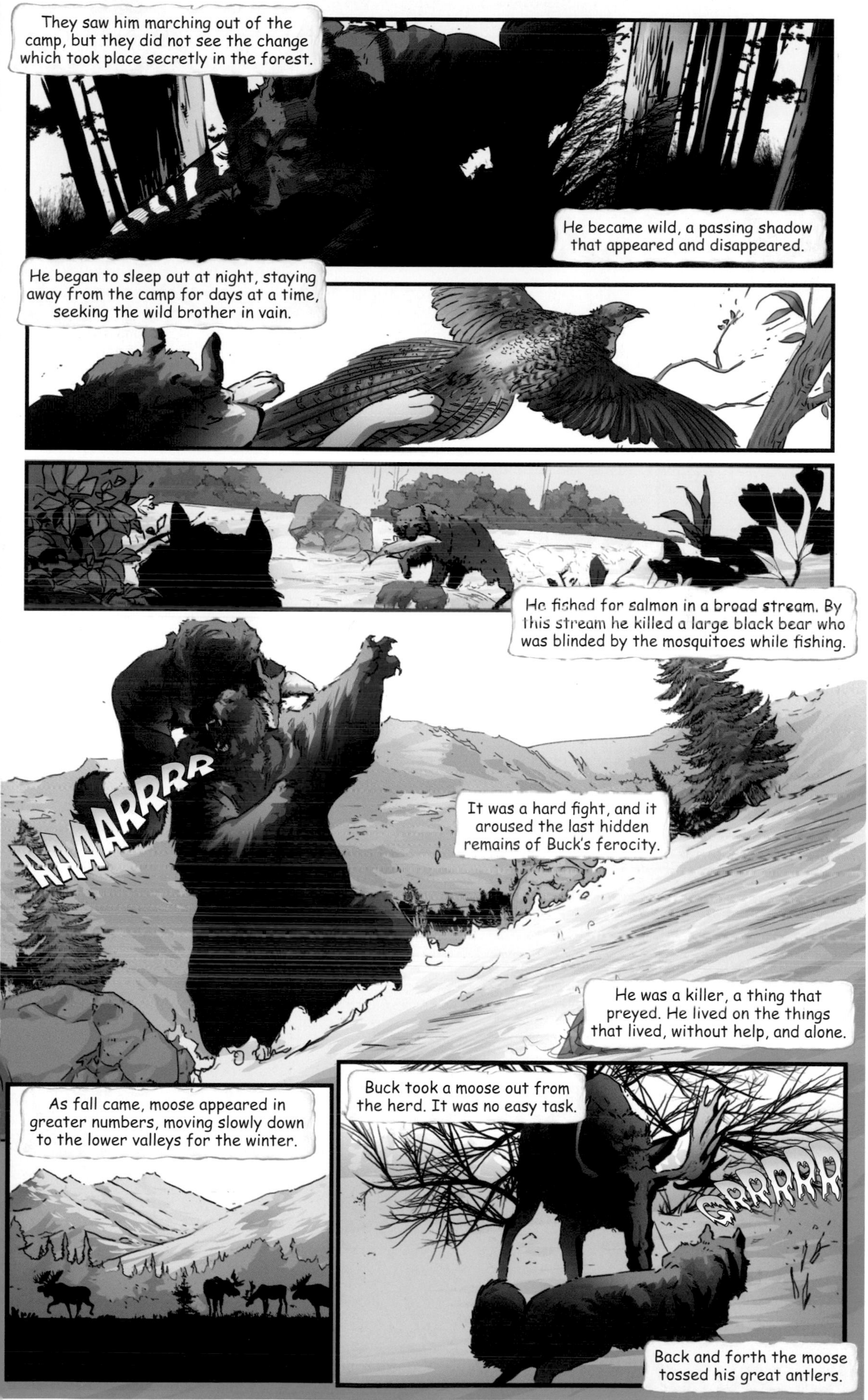
They saw him marching out of the camp, but they did not see the change which took place secretly in the forest.
He became wild, a passing shadow that appeared and disappeared.
He began to sleep out at night, staying away from the camp for days at a time, seeking the wild brother in vain.
He fished for salmon in a broad stream. By this stream he killed a large black bear who was blinded by the mosquitoes while fishing.
AAAARRRR
It was a hard fight, and it aroused the last hidden remains of Buck's ferocity.
He was a killer, a thing that preyed. He lived on the things that lived, without help, and alone.
As fall came, moose appeared in greater numbers, moving slowly down to the lower valleys for the winter.
Buck took a moose out from the herd. It was no easy task.
GRRRRR
Back and forth the moose tossed his great antlers.

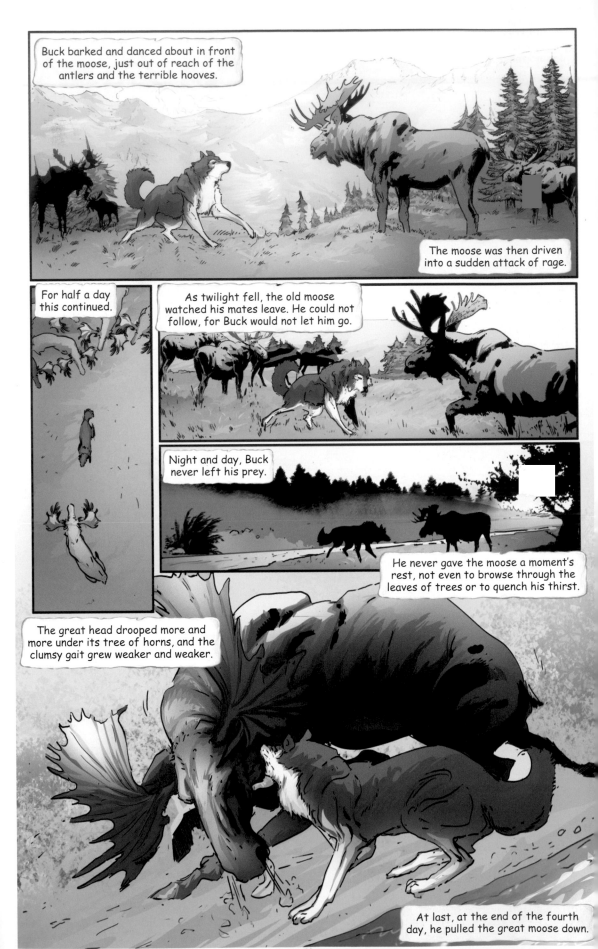

Buck barked and danced about in front of the moose, just out of reach of the antlers and the terrible hooves.

The moose was then driven into a sudden attack of rage.

For half a day this continued.

As twilight fell, the old moose watched his mates leave. He could not follow, for Buck would not let him go.

Night and day, Buck never left his prey.

He never gave the moose a moment's rest, not even to browse through the leaves of trees or to quench his thirst.

The great head drooped more and more under its tree of horns, and the clumsy gait grew weaker and weaker.

At last, at the end of the fourth day, he pulled the great moose down.

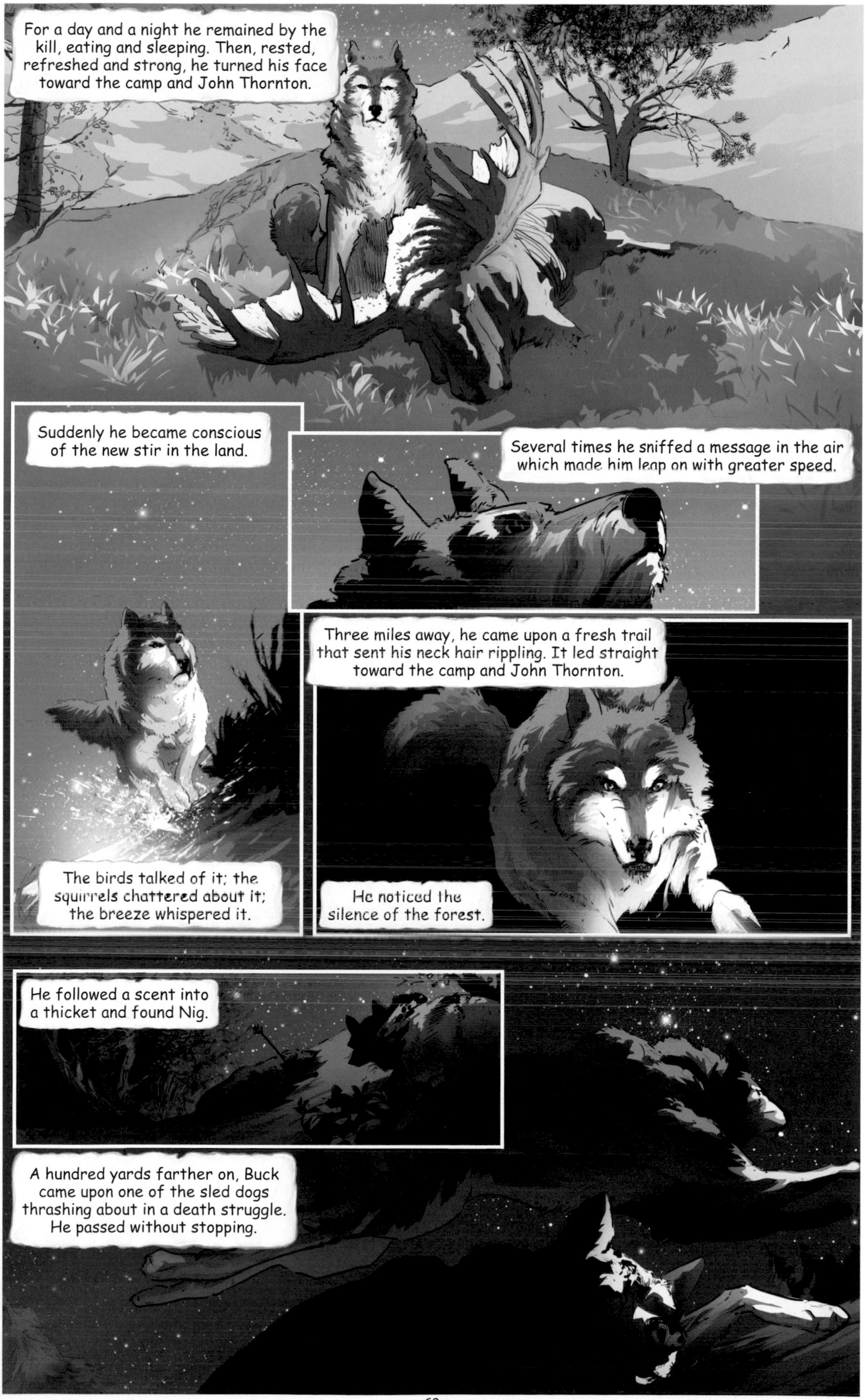
For a day and a night he remained by the kill, eating and sleeping. Then, rested, refreshed and strong, he turned his face toward the camp and John Thornton.
Suddenly he became conscious of the new stir in the land.
Several times he sniffed a message in the air which made him leap on with greater speed.
The birds talked of it; the squirrels chattered about it; the breeze whispered it.
Three miles away, he came upon a fresh trail that sent his neck hair rippling. It led straight toward the camp and John Thornton.
He noticed the silence of the forest.
He followed a scent into a thicket and found Nig.
A hundred yards farther on, Buck came upon one of the sled dogs thrashing about in a death struggle. He passed without stopping.

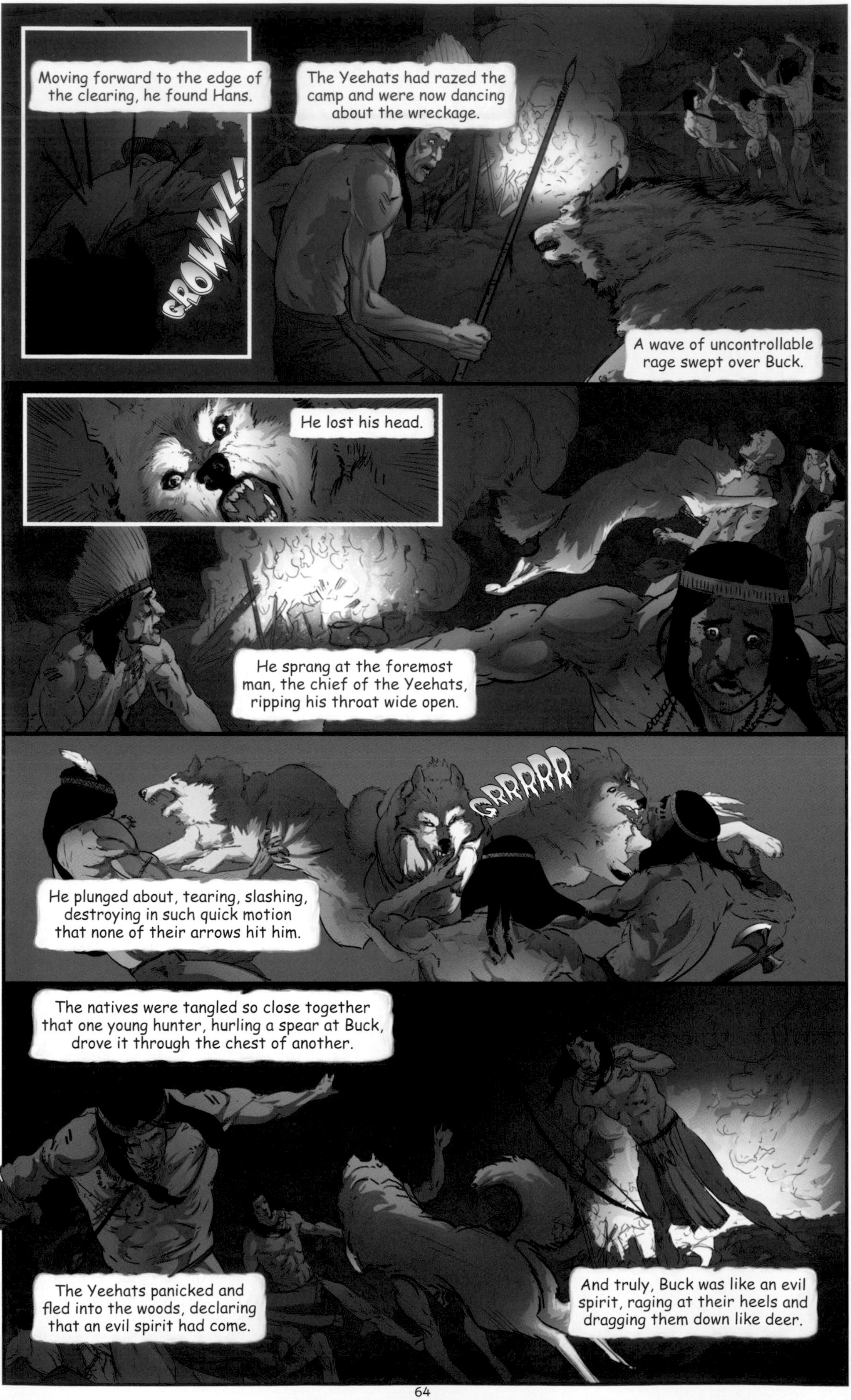
Moving forward to the edge of the clearing, he found Hans.
GROWL!!
The Yeehats had razed the camp and were now dancing about the wreckage.
A wave of uncontrollable rage swept over Buck.
He lost his head.
He sprang at the foremost man, the chief of the Yeehats, ripping his throat wide open.
GRRRRR
He plunged about, tearing, slashing, destroying in such quick motion that none of their arrows hit him.
The natives were tangled so close together that one young hunter, hurling a spear at Buck, drove it through the chest of another.
The Yeehats panicked and fled into the woods, declaring that an evil spirit had come.
And truly, Buck was like an evil spirit, raging at their heels and dragging them down like deer.

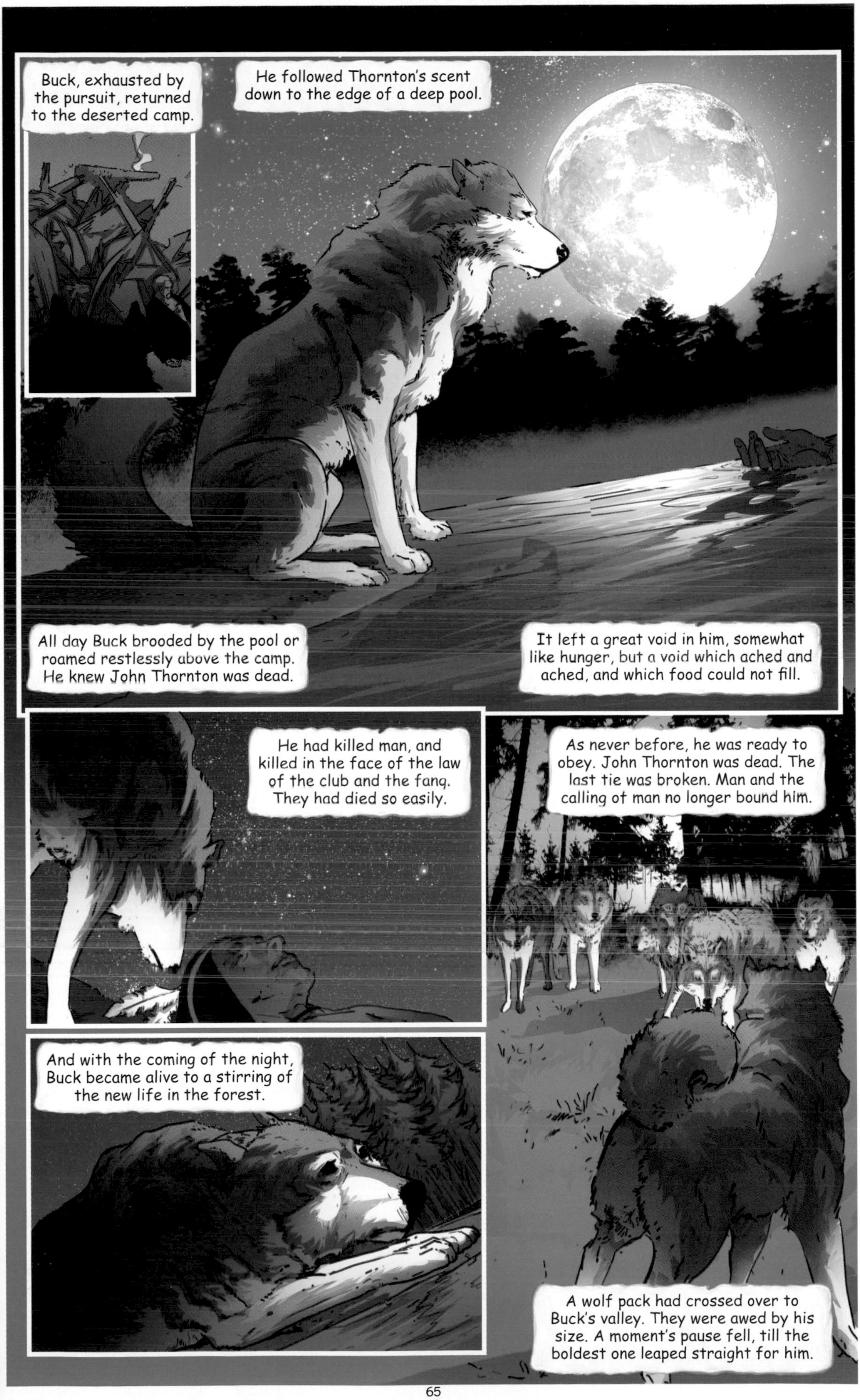

Buck, exhausted by the pursuit, returned to the deserted camp.
He followed Thornton's scent down to the edge of a deep pool.
All day Buck brooded by the pool or roamed restlessly above the camp. He knew John Thornton was dead.
It left a great void in him, somewhat like hunger, but a void which ached and ached, and which food could not fill.
He had killed man, and killed in the face of the law of the club and the fang. They had died so easily.
And with the coming of the night, Buck became alive to a stirring of the new life in the forest.
As never before, he was ready to obey. John Thornton was dead. The last tie was broken. Man and the calling of man no longer bound him.
A wolf pack had crossed over to Buck's valley. They were awed by his size. A moment's pause fell, till the boldest one leaped straight for him.

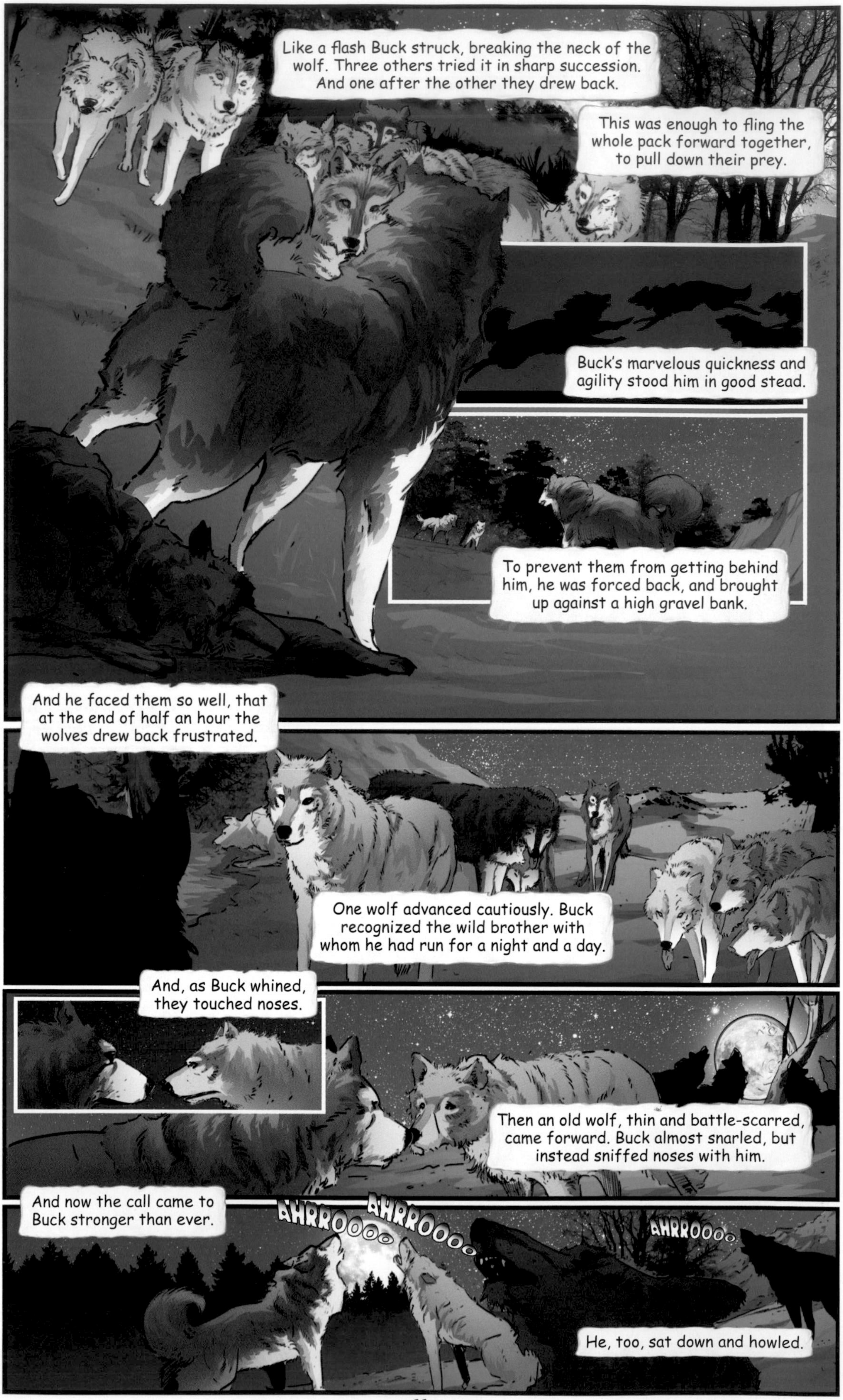
Like a flash Buck struck, breaking the neck of the wolf. Three others tried it in sharp succession. And one after the other they drew back.
This was enough to fling the whole pack forward together, to pull down their prey.
Buck's marvelous quickness and agility stood him in good stead.
To prevent them from getting behind him, he was forced back, and brought up against a high gravel bank.
And he faced them so well, that at the end of half an hour the wolves drew back frustrated.
One wolf advanced cautiously. Buck recognized the wild brother with whom he had run for a night and a day.
And, as Buck whined, they touched noses.
Then an old wolf, thin and battle-scarred, came forward. Buck almost snarled, but instead sniffed noses with him.
And now the call came to Buck stronger than ever.
AHRROOOOO
AHRROOOOO
AHRROOOOO
He, too, sat down and howled.

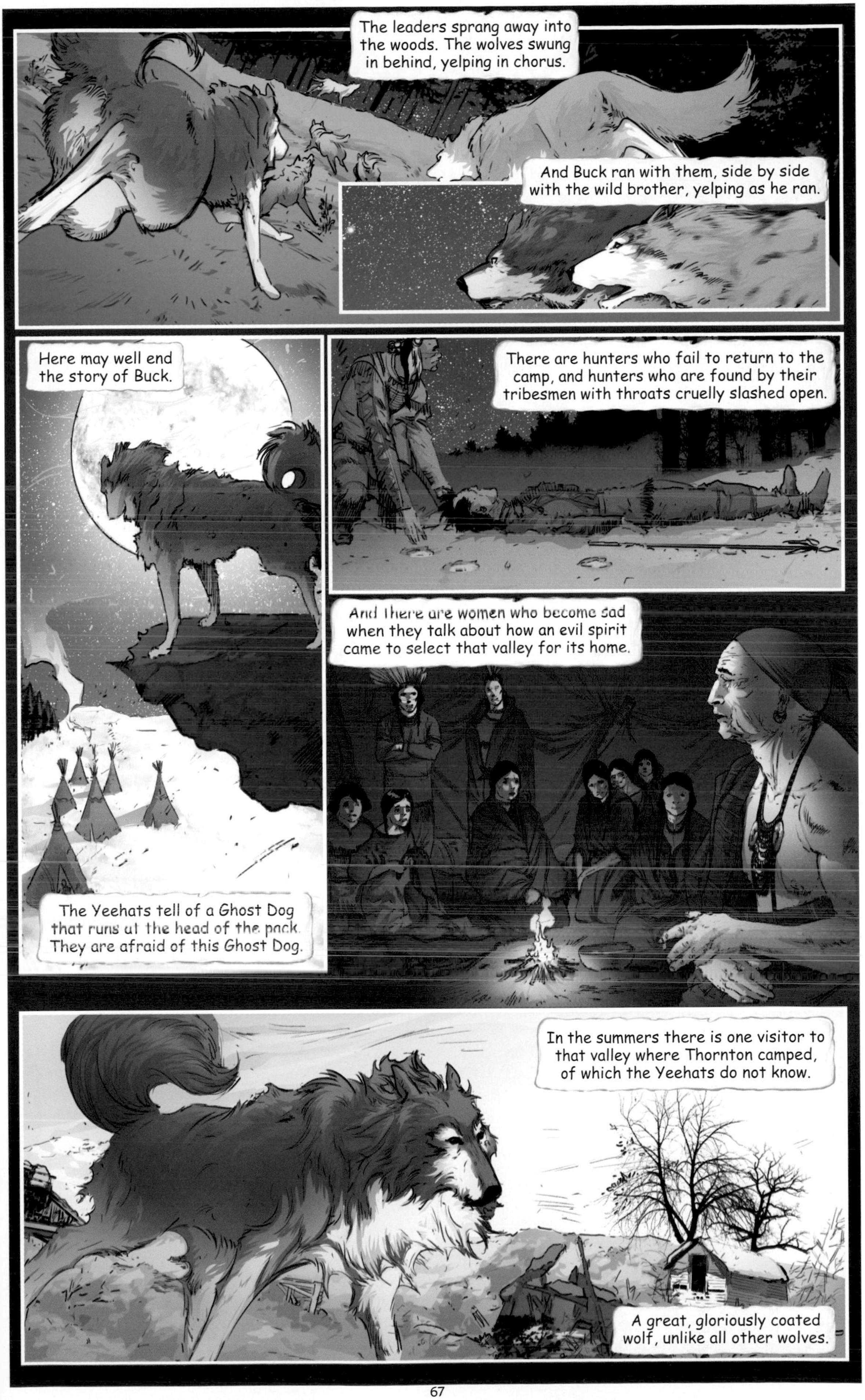

The leaders sprang away into the woods. The wolves swung in behind, yelping in chorus.
And Buck ran with them, side by side with the wild brother, yelping as he ran.
Here may well end the story of Buck.
The Yeehats tell of a Ghost Dog that runs at the head of the pack. They are afraid of this Ghost Dog.
There are hunters who fail to return to the camp, and hunters who are found by their tribesmen with throats cruelly slashed open.
And there are women who become sad when they talk about how an evil spirit came to select that valley for its home.
In the summers there is one visitor to that valley where Thornton camped, of which the Yeehats do not know.
A great, gloriously coated wolf, unlike all other wolves.

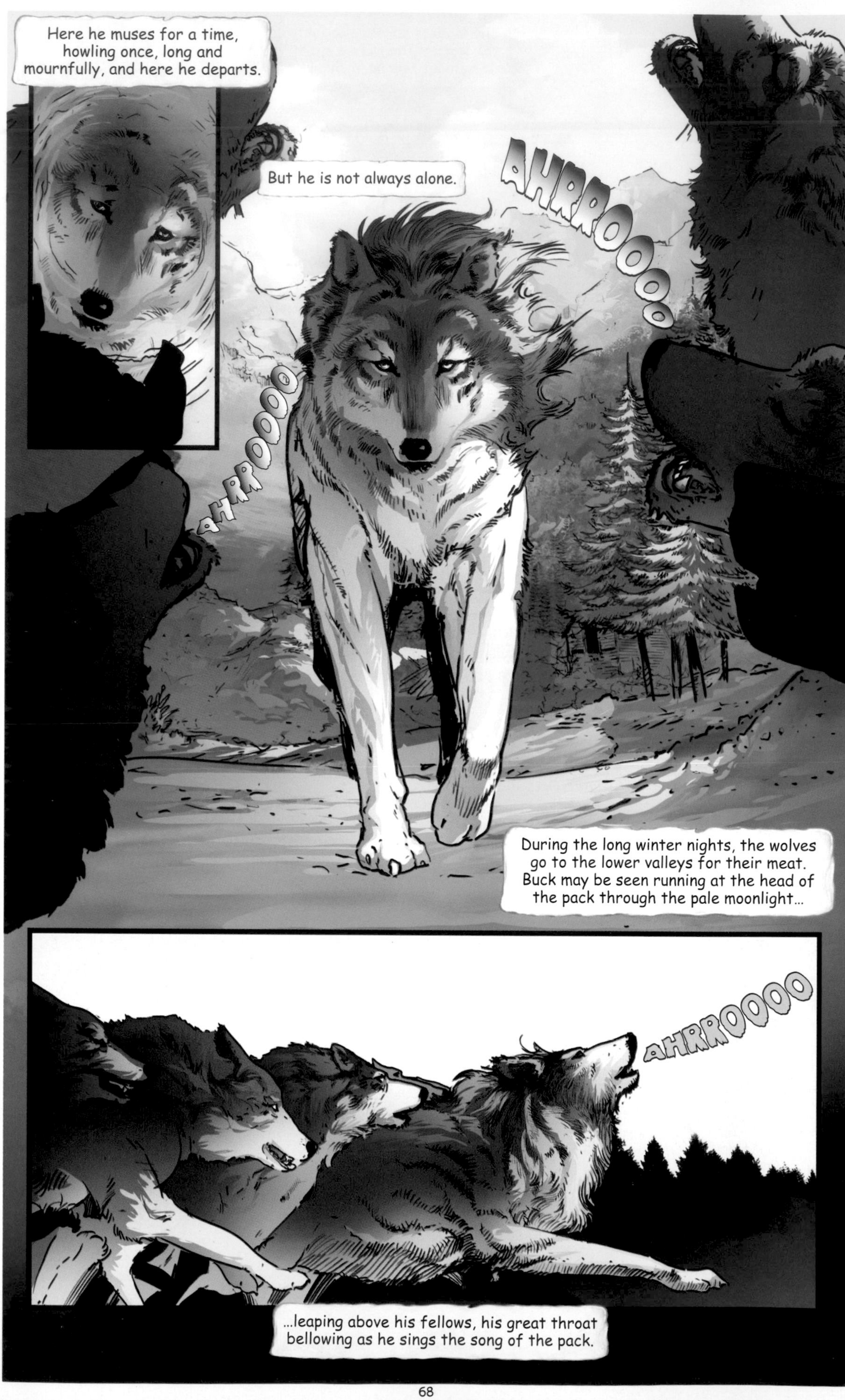
Here he muses for a time, howling once, long and mournfully, and here he departs.
But he is not always alone.
AHRROOOO
AHRROOOO
During the long winter nights, the wolves go to the lower valleys for their meat. Buck may be seen running at the head of the pack through the pale moonlight...
AHRROOOO
...leaping above his fellows, his great throat bellowing as he sings the song of the pack.

# GOLD RUSH

The California Gold Rush was the most significant event of the mid-19th century. People from America, Europe, Asia, and South America rushed here in search of instant wealth. The chance discovery of gold in the riverbed forever changed the simple life into the entrepreneurial, free life that California is today. Some hit it well and made a fortune, some lost everything, including life!

## How was the gold discovered?

John Sutter, a Swiss immigrant, came to California in 1839 with the dream of setting up an agricultural empire. In late 1847, James Marshall who worked in Sutter's saw mill found some shiny metal on the tailrace. Marshall showed the samples to Sutter, and together they tested the shiny metal and found it to be gold. Sutter kept the discovery a secret.

## How did the word about the gold get around?

A man named Sam Brannan ran through the streets of San Francisco with a bottle of gold dust, shouting about Marshall's discovery. This triggered the start of the gold rush. Seeing the rush, Sam Brannan purchased every pickaxe, pan, and shovel in the region and supplied these tools at a high price to the miners. And guess what! In just nine weeks he made thirty-six thousand dollars. He was the richest man during the gold rush, one who did not even mine for gold! Others who made it big during this time were John Studebaker, the pioneer in automobiles, and Henry Wells and William Fargo, the brains behind banking, to name a few. By early 1849, gold fever had become an epidemic. Can you guess what tempted people to rush to California? The fact that gold was free to anyone who could find it. A miner could take 25 to 35 dollars worth of gold a day, or even more out of the riverbed, though actually only the very fortunate people made it really big!

## Did you know ?

The Levi's jeans that you wear almost every day were invented during the gold rush era. The founder, Levi Strauss, designed pants made of canvas for its toughness after he heard complaints from the miners about cotton pants getting torn easily.

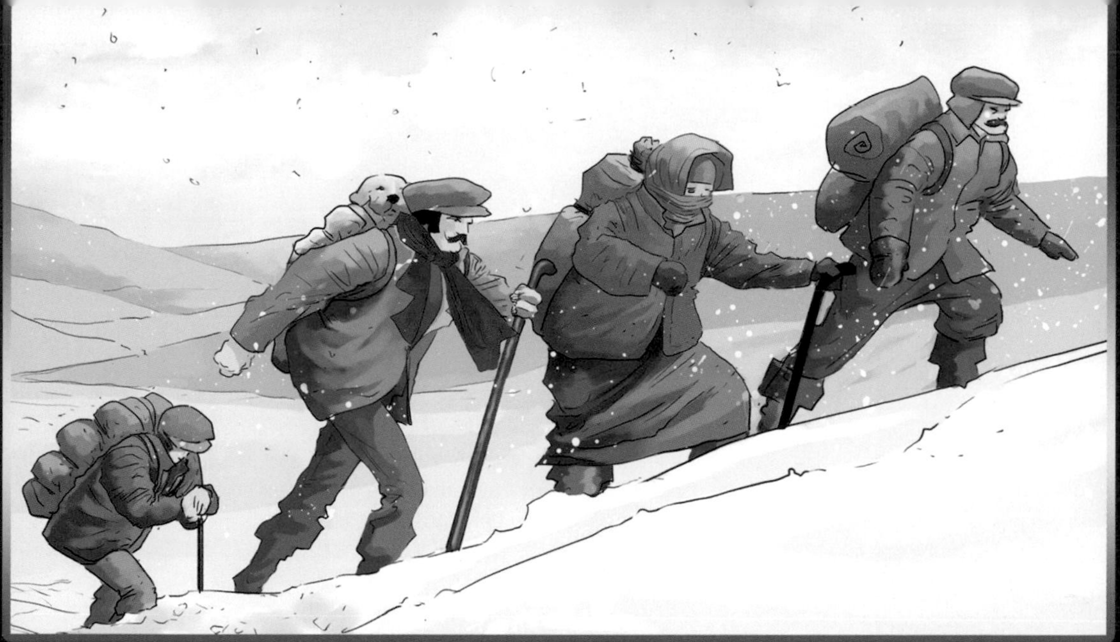

## Klondike gold rush

Klondike, in the Yukon Territory in Canada, was seen as a place where anyone could make his fortune. It drew 100,000 people, all searching for gold. The trail was dangerous, but those who survived it were disappointed. The gold-bearing creeks had already been claimed by the locals before the prospectors had arrived. The much advertized claims of 'gold for the taking' were overstated. Thus, the Klondike gold rush ended as quickly as it had begun. Klondike was immortalized by some of the best writers of the era, like Jack London in *The Call of the Wild*, Robert Service in *The Shooting of Dan McGrew*, and Tappan Adney in *The Klondike Stampede*. Charlie Chaplin's film *The Gold Rush* was also set in Klondike.

**Did you know?**

Mark Twain came to California in the gold rush era as a complete unknown and took a job writing for the newspaper *San Francisco Call*. He was known as Samuel Clemens back then.

The preferred route to the gold fields was over the land and not the sea. Covered wagons were used to carry various items for survival and self-protection.

Would you spend $100 for a glass of water? Unthinkable, isn't it? But the people on their way to California did. A few clever businessmen brought barrels of water to the trail and sold it for as high as $100 a glass to the travelers.

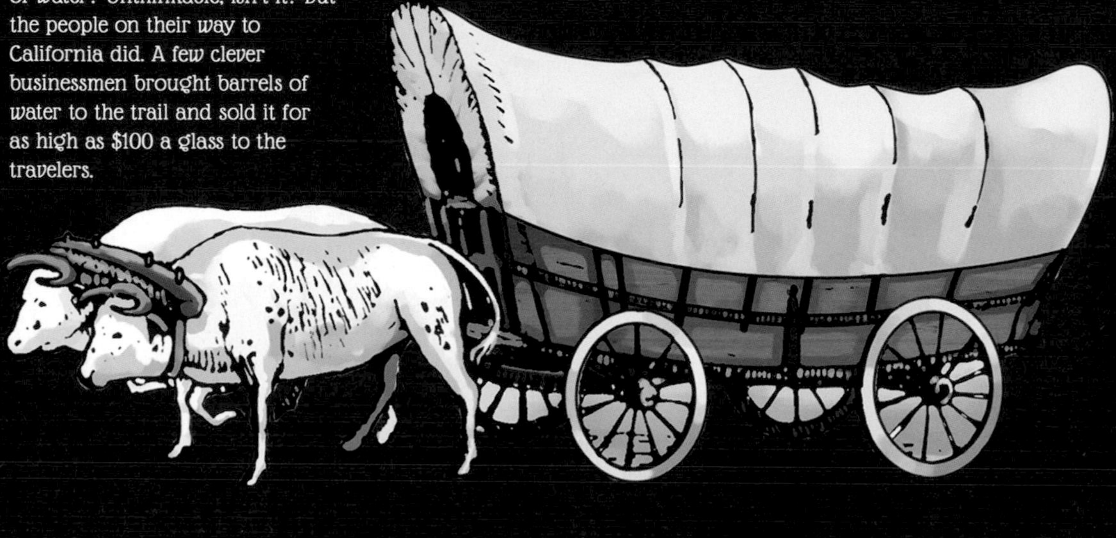

# Classics from CAMPFIRE

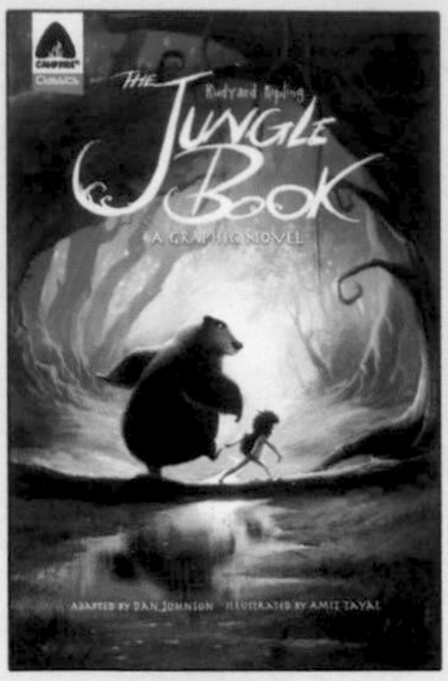
Rudyard Kipling
The Jungle Book
A Graphic Novel

The adventure of a lifetime begins on the night a man-cub called Mowgli, escapes certain doom at the hands of the tiger, Shere Khan. Raised by a wolf pack and taught how to survive by Bagheera, the black panther, and Baloo, the bear, Mowgli comes of age and soon the hunter becomes the hunted as the boy and tiger square off in an epic struggle to the death.

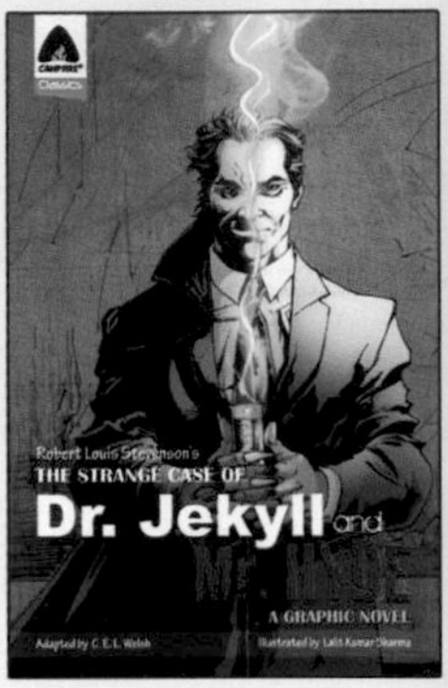
Robert Louis Stevenson's
THE STRANGE CASE OF
Dr. Jekyll and
A GRAPHIC NOVEL

Bold, visionary Henry Jekyll believes he can use his scientific knowledge to divide a person into two beings—one of pure good and one of pure evil. Working tirelessly in his secret laboratory he eventually succeeds—but only halfway. Instead of separating the good and evil halves, Jekyll manages to isolate only the latter. His friends think Jekyll will waste away and fear the worst. Can Jekyll undo what he has done? Or will it change things forever?

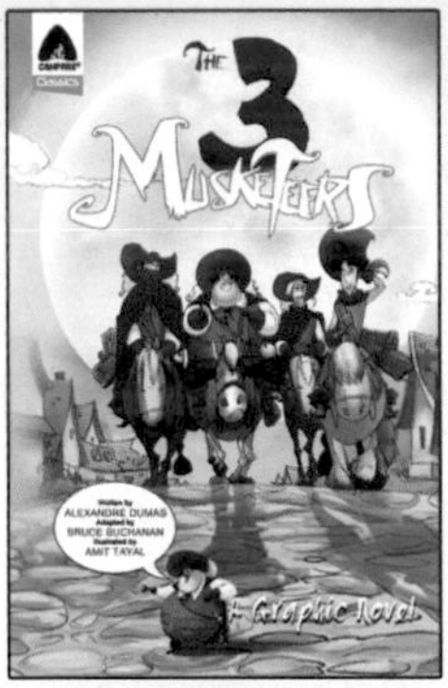
The 3 Musketeers
A Graphic Novel

Young d'Artagnan has only one ambition – to become a king's musketeer. With these dreams, he comes to Paris and befriends Athos, Porthos, and Aramis, the three musketeers and falls in love with Constance, Queen Anne's linen maid. Soon d'Artagnan and his friends find themselves fighting to foil the evil Count Richelieu's plot to disgrace the Queen.

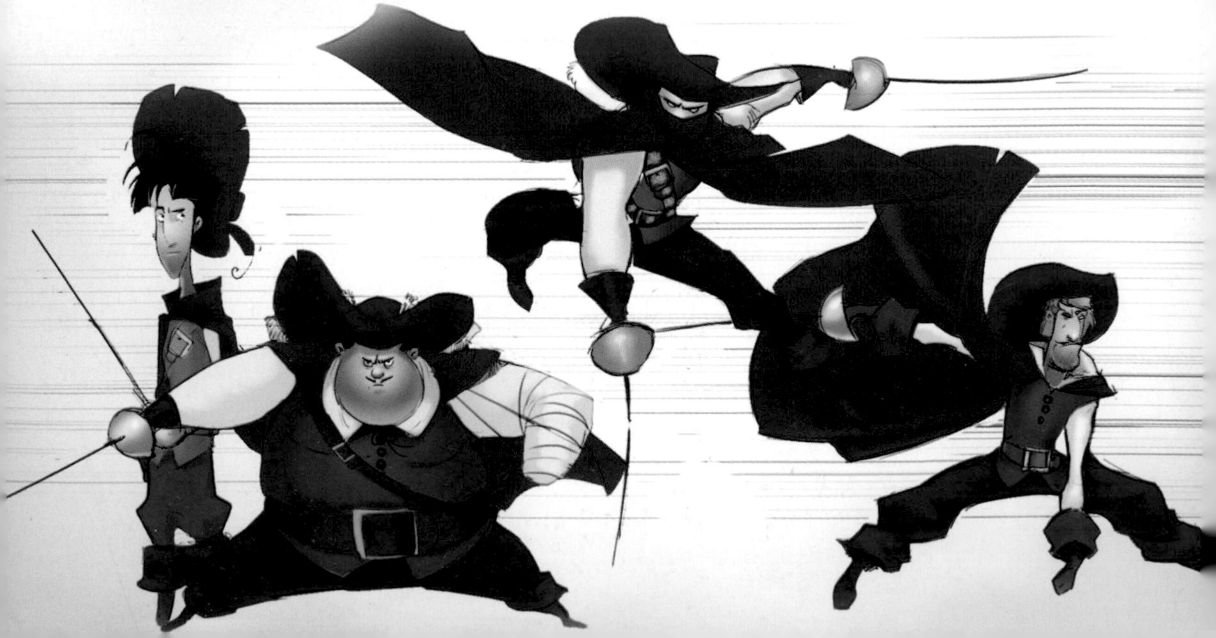